TIME
AND
TIME AGAIN

THE CURIOUS CASE OF MR. STEPHEN WHITE

J.B. HOGAN

ALSO BY

J.B. HOGAN

MEXICAN SKIES

TIN HOLLOW

FALLEN: A SHORT STORY COLLECTION

THE RUBICON: POETRY AND SHORT FICTION

LOSING COTTON

LIVING BEHIND TIME

ANGELS IN THE OUTFIELD

THE APOSTATE

TIME
AND
TIME AGAIN

THE CURIOUS CASE OF MR. STEPHEN WHITE

J.B. HOGAN

FLEET

OGHMA CREATIVE MEDIA

www.oghmacreative.com

ISBN: 978-1-63373-335-0

Interior Design by Casey W. Cowan
Editing by Gordon Bonnet

Fleet Press
Oghma Creative Media
Bentonville, Arkansas
www.oghmacreative.com

To Larry Fultz,
because we found the first cave.

And to Casey Cowan,
for all the hard work and the great covers.

TIME AND TIME AGAIN

THE CURIOUS CASE OF MR. STEPHEN WHITE

CAVER

Stephen White didn't think of himself as much of a caver. He had a touch of claustrophobia and the musty, sometimes dusty, sometimes moldy, cave air often made it difficult for him to breathe. He preferred caves in which you could crawl around on your hands and knees—at the very least.

He actually didn't think there was anything wrong with finding a cave in which you could walk hunched over, maybe even stand upright. He knew other cavers thought that was kind of weird—they all seemed to like squeezing through the tiniest holes in the world and then barely being able to get back out.

Stephen didn't like that approach much, even though he knew the reward could be an incredible room filled with crystal formations or some other such wondrous thing, and so he did the one thing most smart cavers don't do: he usually went caving by himself.

On a quiet Saturday morning in early October, under a clear blue sky and a bright, not warm sun, solitary Stephen clambered up a steep bluff above the Marais des Cygnes River in a woody region not so far from the Kansas border. He was headed toward what he hoped, and had been led to believe by his work buddy Tom Harris back in Nevada, Missouri, was a seldom-disturbed cave far enough away from the normal haunts to not be frequented by the usual crowd of local spelunking enthusiasts.

Tom had told him that there might be Indian points in the cave as well and had sworn he'd seen lots of flint and even some evidence of old fire remains on a brief visit to the cave some months back. He had reassured Stephen that the cave was a "primo" spot and that only other opportunities had kept him, Tom, from returning himself.

Breathing loudly, Stephen hoisted his twenty pounds or so overweight body up the rocky, leaf-covered bluff while nearby jays chattered angrily at his loud progress into their territory. Squirrels hopped around the trees and a few remaining insects occasionally buzzed by his head. He paused for a drink of water from a hard plastic bottle and wiped the sweat off his forehead with the bottom of his worn sweatshirt.

For a moment he considered digging in his backpack for the raw mushroom and soy cheese sandwich he had brought for his lunch but decided to forego that pleasure at least until he had found the new cave—if he did. He had harvested and thoroughly cleaned the mushrooms himself and was anxious to dig into their meaty texture as soon as possible.

Resuming his scramble, he labored along the bluff, traversing its difficult terrain from east to west. He could feel his big toes straining against the ends of his new hiking boots and realized he had ordered them one-half size too small. He had purchased them online from a site that Lisa Backman, the beautiful software engineer Stephen not so secretly adored at work, had recommended. Now he felt his mind straining against the emotional edges of the regret building in him if he had to admit to Lisa that he would have to exchange the new boots even after she had helped him pick them out.

Chugging across the bluff imagining Lisa's green eyes, wavy brown hair, tight buttocks, and full round breasts—breasts that strained against her blouses like his toes strained against his new boots—Stephen perspired profusely. He stopped to wipe sweat beads off his thick wire-rim glasses. When he put the glasses back on, there was the cave. Or at least what looked like a cave through the gray branches of the thick, dying underbrush.

"Hot damn," he exclaimed, anticipating his discovery. "Old Tom was right. There is a cave."

With a final burst of energy he quickly made his way towards what looked like the cave's entrance. And it was a cave. A cave with a wide opening. Stephen scrabbled over rocks, leaves, and small green ferns in his last, puffing approach to the cave.

"All right." He stopped at the cave entrance to catch his breath.

The cave entrance was maybe twenty-five feet across and more than six feet high at its tallest vertical point just off center of the opening. The ground immediately inside was dry and of a bright brown hue. It looked soft enough to dig easily in. He could see back into the cave at least forty or fifty feet before it faded into darkness.

That didn't trouble him. He had brought his headlamp and, of course, his knee pads. He always had his knee pads. And he had remembered to bring a small pick for digging and a little trowel for fine work. As soon as he munched his sandwich—he had worked up a good appetite from all that hiking—he would explore to his heart's content.

After eating his sandwich—devouring it was perhaps more apt—and taking a good long drink of water to flush the dry bread and mushrooms down his throat, Stephen donned the headlamp and knee pads. He pulled out the pick and trowel in case he found something promising and set to work. It turned out to be a good cave.

Within ten minutes he had found several intriguing flakes and he cheered with delight moments later when an edge he unearthed with his boot turned out to be the broken end of a human-worked piece of flint so large it must have been a spear point. Invigorated by his find, Stephen kept digging and working his way further back into the cave finding more and more flakes and an occasional broken point. He was sure he was going to find something really good really soon.

Sure enough he did. Near the narrowing, low back of the primary cave—he could see there were more rooms beyond this front section—he popped up a small piece of rock and it was a beautiful, fully worked point. An arrowhead. Big enough to use on large animals, or men. Stephen let out an echoing whoop and rapidly rubbed the dirt off the point with his thumb and forefinger.

It was a real beauty, made of a brownish flint and complete with nicely formed notches and finely honed edges. It was, as Tom might say, a primo point, worth the entire trip itself. Stephen, who also was an amateur historian of the area, placed the arrowhead in a relatively recent epoch, when the area of the Marais des Cygnes had been inhabited exclusively by indigenous peoples.

Thrilled with his discovery, he pocketed the arrowhead and adjusted his headlamp in preparation for the exploration of the back room, or maybe rooms, behind the main cave. Then, just as he reached to click on his lamp it happened. At first he thought he might have gotten some dust in his eyes, but after he wiped them with his sweatshirt he saw it again.

Flashes at first, then shadows. The hair on the back of his neck stood up. He froze in his progress towards the back of the cave. The shadows became more pronounced, began to take shape. He felt his throat constrict and his head suddenly felt hot and sweaty. His legs wobbled and he felt nauseated, disoriented. The shadows flitted by, raced by, seemingly in all directions. He slumped down, feeling sick and terrified.

He closed his eyes hoping to make sense of things but when he opened them the shadows had become forms—forms he began to recognize. They were pigs or at least some sort of wild peccary, and they appeared to be running along the walls. Stephen closed his eyes again and opened them. The pigs were racing by now on either side of him. He could almost touch them but they seemed ethereal, like holograms.

In a moment, the pigs were gone. He shook his head, as if some mental cobwebs had gotten in there and messed up his thought processes. He wanted to stand but found he couldn't. He simply sat there in the dirt of the cave floor. Then more images came rumbling out of the cave, into the cave. There were other animals, deer, bear, small creatures, too, like raccoon and possum. Then taller images. Upright images. Stephen held his breath. These were men.

Short men came through the cave, hologram-like still, and went about the business of cave living. They built fires, they brought in game, cooked it, ate it. They danced around bent over, whooped silent calls, drew images on the cave walls. Stephen slowly rose at last, stood up, as well as he could there in the back of the cave. The cave people went about their business. He was invisible to them. And then they were gone. Only animal images again and Stephen waited on gradually steadying knees, for what he didn't know.

After some time, men came again into the cave. Men he could see clearly now. Native men. Men with long hair, men with animal claw and tooth necklaces—and women, too. He saw them chanting without sound, dancing without song, living without solid form. Then they too were gone. The images were gone. But a new sensation began. He was sure he could now hear sounds in the back of the cave. Sounds that were familiar. And smells. He could smell coffee and the aroma of bacon cooked on an open fire. And suddenly they were all around him. Talking, laughing, arguing.

There were maybe a dozen. Twelve young men. Dirty, poorly dressed, ragged, so thin their coats hung on them outsized. He was right in the middle of them. They did not seem to notice him. He pulled away to the side of the cave. Watched. Listened in awe, in shock. Who were they? What were they?

They seemed real now, corporeal. No longer holograms or perhaps something in between. He heard them talking. They called one tall, wild-eyed young man Bill. He seemed to be their leader. He gestured crazily with his hands and arms. He appeared highly agitated. Stephen listened, he was beginning to hear the man's words ever more clearly, all the men's words.

He feared they would see him, turn on him. They were all armed, as he had read described in many books, to the teeth. Every man seemed to have at least four pistols on his person, mostly tucked behind belts or ropes worn as belts. But they took no notice of Stephen, did not seem to see him.

"They took our womenfolk," he could now hear the wild-eyed leader say, "and we're goin' to do somethin' about it."

"What about Q.?" A tall boy, wearing a hat with a large bird feather in it, said. "Shouldn't we wait for him?"

"Yeah." A short, thick-boned man pointed at the boy with the feather in his hat, "Jimmy's right. We need to wait for Q."

"William will not be here for mebbe a week," the one called Bill said. "I'm in command. And I say we are gonna take revenge and take it now."

"Bill is right." A broad-shouldered man came forward to stand by the leader, "Q. and Jesse are plumb off near Sedalia. It could be days before they get back. We make these damnable Jayhawkers pay, now."

"Is there enough of us, Frank?" the thick-boned man said to the broad-shouldered man.

"There's plenty, Bates," Frank answered with authority. "And there's time, if we ride now."

"I don't know." Jimmy sounded doubtful.

"If you ain't got the stomach for it," Bill said harshly.

"Jimmy's got the gumption," Frank intervened for the boy. "He just ain't used to ridin' without Q., are you, boy?"

"No, sir."

"All you have to do," Frank eased the boy's concern, "is keep the extra horses in line. The remuda, like we learned about down in Indian Territory, remember? Don't get spooked, or jumpy."

"Yes, sir, Frank. I can do it, too."

"You bet you can. Be sure to bring plenty of extra pistols, powder, and bullets."

"Yes, sir."

"All right, by God." Bill waved an arm with the index finger pointing at them "Get stuff ready. We're ridin' now."

Stephen, still in near shock at the scene before him, clung to a wall, watched the marauders—Border Ruffians, he knew from his history books—preparing for a raid. The men gathered pistols, gunpowder, caps, bullets, knives, all the necessary implements of war from a box buried toward the back side of the cave opposite where Stephen stood mesmerized.

After each man was ready, the group moved toward the front of the cave. Stephen edged along the far wall, still fearful these hard-looking men would spot him. He did not understand what was happening but curiosity got the better of him and he followed the group back to the cave entrance.

Outside, the boy Jimmy had brought up the horses, including four extras and a smaller one following its mother, that would make up the marauder's remuda. The leader Bill circled the men up for a last word.

"There will be no captives," he told his men, a grim smile on his face. "That ain't what we intend this time."

"We cain't just shoot 'em down like dogs, can we?" Bates, the thick-boned man, said.

"No prisoners," Bill countered. "None."

"This is a war, boys." Frank looked at Jimmy and Bates in particular. "We cain't ride with captives."

"Kill 'em all," Bill growled. "Remember our women."

"Amen," Frank agreed.

"Let's go," Bill commanded, and the men mounted as one.

The marauders took off away from the cave, Jimmy following with the remuda. The smaller horse hung back, confused for a moment, and Stephen ran to it and jumped onto its back. The horse reared and whinnied, raised its front legs. Stephen grabbed its mane and held on for dear life. The horse bolted after the others, chasing its mother.

Stephen estimated that the ride took just over thirty minutes. He knew they were riding west because he could see the sun ahead of him in the sky. They had stayed along the banks of the Marais des Cygnes and finally slowed up when they reached a flat area with large, open fields on either side of the river. The leader Bill signaled for the others to rein in and the group moved away from the river and into a small grove of trees.

"They's right over there in a farmhouse," he told his marauders. "We go in fast and hard and take 'em. If they resist, shoot 'em dead."

"Ain't we gonna give 'em a chance?" Jimmy said timorously.

"They didn't give none of such to our women," Bill snarled at the boy. "They'll get none in return."

"But these ain't the same ones..." Jimmy began.

"If you're yellow," Bill growled, "go on home now. To your momma."

"I ain't none of that." Jimmy countered.

"Then let's go;" Bill said.

"Head 'em out," Frank called from his position behind Bill. "Check your pistols and powder. Got your caps?" All the men had. "Then ride on. Get the Jayhawkers." Frank said.

Stephen hung on for dear life again to the little horse's mane as the Border Ruffians stormed out of the woods and encircled a small farmhouse. The assault was so fast, so unexpected by the occupants, that within moments the marauders held four men and a young woman hostage.

"Take 'em back down by the river," Bill told his troops.

The marauders drug their captives by rope to the banks of the Marais des Cygnes where Bill held a colloquy with them.

"Are you Unionists?" he waving a pistol before them.

The captives, unsure what to say, unsure who these armed men were, tried to avoid an answer.

"We are farmers," the oldest of the group, a man of about forty years of age said. "That's all."

"For the Union?" Bill said again, then added: "Or for the Confederacy?"

The terrified men tried to tell from their captors' ragged clothes and partial uniforms which side they represented. There was no way to know.

"Union?" the older man said.

"That's it," Bill said coldly.

"Why are you doing this?" the girl cried. "We've done nothing to you. We just want to live in peace."

"Move her out of the way, Bates," Frank told the thick-boned raider.

Bates grabbed the girl and drug her kicking and screaming away from the captured men.

"Leave my sister alone, you bastards," a younger captive yelled at Bates.

The young man stepped toward Bates and his sister. At the same moment, Bill fired one of his pistols at point blank range, dropping the young boy.

"Tommy," the girl cried out, struggling against Bates' strong grip.

Suddenly, the marauders lost all discipline. They fired with abandon into the remaining captives. The sound was deafening and smoke filled the air around the river. When the shooting stopped, the four captives were dead on the ground, riddled with bullets. The girl, sobbing loudly, had slumped to her knees in the grass. Bates held onto her with one hand. She did not struggle to escape.

"Jesus," Jimmy stared at the scene of carnage before him, then looked to his fellow marauders, "oh, Jesus."

"What do we do with this here girl?" Bates called out into the smoky silence.

"Let me have her," a tall, skinny boy who had fired on the captives from the back of the marauder gang. "I'll take care of her."

Stephen, still astride the little pony and near the tall boy, was nearly in a state of shock from witnessing the murders but he couldn't bear to see anything happen to this girl. She was pretty, in a familiar way, and brave and it was more than he could stand. Whatever was happening, he wasn't going to allow these killers to harm her. Leaping off the pony, he ran at the tall boy and took a swing at him—but his arm went right through the boy. A dream, Stephen instantly thought, this is a dream. But the boy Jimmy reacted.

"Watch out," he called over to the tall boy, simultaneously pulling a pistol from his belt.

"Hey," the tall boy yelled, ducking and jerking his own pony forward, "don't point that thing at me. What the hell's the matter with you?"

"I thought I seen somethin'." Jimmy said, confused.

"You boys calm down," Frank warned the young men, "'fore somebody gets shot."

"And let the girl go," Bill told Bates. "Let her be. We don't harm no women."

"Damn you bastards," the girl cried when Bates released her. "You murderin', evil bastards. I hope you rot in hell."

"We no doubt will, miss," Bill told her, "we no doubt will. Now, head 'em out, boys," he told his gang, "back to Missouri."

The marauders turned their horses and trotted them back down the banks of the Marais des Cygnes. The girl ran to the bodies of the men and threw herself on them crying inconsolably. Stephen remained for a moment watching the girl, but she never looked up. In profile, he was sure she was someone he knew. Someone he knew well. He started to reach for her but stopped. He realized the girl had no idea he was there.

Grabbing and remounting the little pony, Stephen let the animal guide itself in the direction the marauders had gone. The little horse had a strong homing device and didn't like being away from the other mounts, especially its mother. Still, by the time Stephen and the little horse reached the cave again, the band of outlaws were already back and settling in. A fire had been started and something like a stew was being prepared in a big, black iron pot above the flames.

"Jimmy," Bates called from the cave entrance, "the little yearling is back."

"Boy, that's good. That little horse was really actin' funny today. I swear I seen somethin' on him one time."

"Yeah, and you damned near shot me 'cause of it," the tall boy reminded him.

"I'm awful sorry 'bout that, Gardner."

"Nothin' for it," Gardner said.

"You boys cut the jawin'," Bill came up to Jimmy and the others. Jimmy wouldn't look at Bill. "You hear me?"

"Yes, sir." Bates and Gardner busied themselves with other work.

"What about you, boy?" Bill addressed Jimmy directly. "You understand me?"

"I understand you."

"You got somethin' to say?"

"There weren't no need to kill them men like that." Jimmy still didn't look up.

"Boy, this is war."

"They was farmers," Jimmy raised his head. "Like us."

"Maybe you are too 'fine'," Bill said harshly, "maybe you don't belong here."

As Jimmy framed a retort, Stephen suddenly felt a chill run down his spine. He jumped and moved in the direction of the arguing men. Jimmy seemed to see the motion and went for one of his pistols. Bill saw the boy's move and went for his.

"Look out, Bill," Jimmy yelled and the commander dodged to his left.

Jimmy aimed his pistol directly where Stephen stood. Stephen tried to cry out and threw up his hands. The last thing he heard was the booming of the black powder revolver. The last thing he saw was the wild look in the Jimmy's eyes.

When Stephen awoke it was nearly completely dark in the cave. He was flat of his back and his head hurt badly. It seemed as if his eyes were going to explode out of their sockets. He sat up gingerly, holding his head with both hands.

"Oh," he moaned, rubbing his eyes.

Then, remembering his last waking moment, he forced his eyes fully open and struggled to his knees. He expected at any moment to be shot by the marauders. He crawled as fast as he could on his hands and knees toward the cave entrance. But there was no need, there was no one in the cave but himself. He stopped and turned on his headlamp. Looking back, where all the fantastic shapes and events had occurred, there was no sign whatsoever of anything ever having been there.

"My God, what was that?" Stephen said to the empty cave.

He struggled on toward the cave entrance, stumbled to his feet near the opening and staggered out into the fresh air. He breathed deeply the humid, river-moist air. It was late in the day. The sun was low on the western horizon. After a moment his head began to clear and his breath came easier, slower, calmer. He was going to be all right.

"Wait'll I tell Tom and Lisa about this," he said out loud. "They'll never believe it. Tom will…."

He paused at the second utterance of Tom's name. Other names and images rushed back to him. Bill, the marauders' leader, Frank and Jimmy, Bates, Gardner. The dead Jayhawkers. The girl crying beside her murdered brother. The little pony. Good heavens, he thought, the stash of guns and ammo. Without hesitation, he turned and practically ran back into the cave.

He hurried past the main portion of the underground lair, repositioned himself where the fantastic events had seemed to transpire. Yes, he thought, right about here. And over there, that's where the guns and other things had been kept. Reaching into his bag, Stephen took out his digging implements and headed for where he had seen the boy Jimmy stash the marauders' bullets, powder, and weaponry.

In less than a quarter hour of searching and digging, he hit something solid with the small pick. He excavated the area carefully and then used the trowel to finish up. About a foot or so below the cave surface it was there. The rotted remains of a wooden box. Stephen carefully scooped out the area. There didn't seem to be anything left. They must've taken everything at some time after the Kansas raid. Left nothing. But just as he was about to give up, the trowel made contact with something else metal.

"Oh, Lord." Stephen's breath caught.

He dug quickly now, but carefully. Then he found it. Removing dirt and mud from the metal object, Stephen held it up to the light of his headlamp. It was an old revolver. A black powder, Civil War era weapon. The caps, if they had ever been there, were long since decomposed but pistol balls were still in the cylinder.

"Man, oh, man," Stephen exclaimed, "wait'll the guys see this one."

He checked around some more but found nothing else. That did not bother him. Whatever had happened here in the cave had led him to this historical prize. He carefully placed the pistol into his backpack and then smoothed the dirt and rocks back over the area where he had dug to find it.

Crawling, then walking, Stephen made his way out of the cave. It was completely dark outside now but he had the headlamp and used it to make his way back to his car. He couldn't wait to get back to town and show Tom the pistol. He wasn't sure he would tell him about the other things that he had seen in the cave, they seemed too fantastical even to him to relate to others.

He would have liked to tell Lisa about the farm girl, though. There was something there about the two women that Stephen couldn't quite get a handle on. And he would need some time to process the visions he'd had. They seemed so real. The marauder boy Jimmy, at least, had apparently sensed him in the other world, had even shot at him.

That was hard to explain all right. But for the time being Stephen wouldn't worry about it. He had found the cave and could return to it any time he wished. He felt it might have other treasures hidden inside—further back, back into some of its deeper rooms.

Next time, he told himself, I'll leave earlier, bring more food. Maybe not fresh mushrooms but something good, and enough of it to spend all the time needed to explore the cave. As he drove back to town, he was feeling really good. Work didn't seem like such a bad thing at the moment. Life was good. He had the cave and he would go back to it again. Soon.

HOLY WAFER

Stephen White was a lapsed Catholic. So lapsed, in fact, that he had not attended mass in over five years. He knew he should go to mass and soon.

"I need to go to mass," he said out loud in his cubicle at Animatec, "and soon."

"What did you say, Stephen." Lisa Backman peered over at him from her adjacent cubicle in the second floor software engineers' bullpen area of the Animatec building just off the square in Nevada, Missouri.

"What... what?" Stephen muttered, embarrassed. "Did I say something out loud?"

"You said you had to go to mass soon, or something like that."

"Oh."

"I didn't know you were a Catholic."

"Uh, yeah." Stephen gazed into Lisa's beautiful light green eyes, feeling their gaze on the pasty whiteness of his sun-starved face. "I am. I mean I was. I guess I still am."

"You don't sound so sure," Lisa said kindly.

"I'm sure," Stephen averted his eyes. He was so enamored of her that he was afraid if he looked at her too long she would see how he really felt and stop being his friend. That would be more than Stephen could bear. "I'm just bad about going to mass."

"How long has it been?"

"I don't know, maybe two, uh, three or four years. Something like that. I need to go to confession. I need to take communion."

"What would you have to confess? You don't ever do anything bad."

"Oh, my God. You don't need to be a murderer to sin, you know."

"Well, go to confession then."

"I'd feel foolish now, after all this time."

"You shouldn't feel foolish about your faith," Lisa said.

"No?" Stephen wondered.

"I'm not Catholic," Lisa acknowledged, "but I bet they would welcome you back without a word. Besides, they wouldn't know how long it had been since you last confessed or took communion would they?"

"At confession they would."

"Maybe you should just do one thing at a time, then," Lisa suggested. "Ease back into it."

"You are so smart, Lisa." His true feelings for her boiled up dangerously close to the surface. She went back to work in her cubicle. "I mean, thanks."

"No problem."

Stephen could hear her keyboard softly clicking away. He sighed deeply and went back to his own work.

—

Stephen went to the ten o'clock mass at his local church the next Sunday, but it wasn't an easy thing for him to do. He stood outside the heavy wooden front doors for close to ten minutes before he could work up the courage to enter. Many worshipers passed him by, giving him odd glances as he stood there shifting his weight from foot to foot.

He was afraid they all knew of his sins. Knew how bad he was. And he was afraid to face the priests now that he had gone to confession. He was sure they would all be able to look out into the crowd and see him—the biggest sinner of all. He had gone to confession Saturday afternoon and spilled his guts, at least the last five years of living guts anyway.

"Bless me father," he had said upon entering the confessional booth, "for I have sinned."

"Tell me about it," the hidden priest's voice seemed filled with sarcasm.

And he did tell the priest about it, all of it. How he had taken the Lord's name in vain, failed to honor his father and mother, touched himself—frequently—and thought bunches of impure thoughts, though he never mentioned Lisa by name.

At the end, he was sure he heard the priest yawn and then declare a lenient ten Hail Marys and ten Our Fathers as penance. He fairly leapt from the booth at the end and immediately did his penance.

Now it was Sunday, the next day, and he was filtering into the church with the other worshippers, already feeling guilty and sinful. Finding a mostly empty pew towards the back of the church, he sat down with a deep sigh.

Contrary to his expectations, mass went just fine. He easily remembered all the correct responses when the priest cued the believers and he did his genuflections with the others and at the appropriate times. By the end he was feeling good and when it was time for communion, he went to the front of the church with some aplomb and confidence.

Kneeling devoutly, he opened his mouth like a little bird when it was his turn to take the holy wafer, the body of his Lord. He closed his eyes when the priest hovered over him and placed the thin, white wafer directly onto his tongue.

He closed his mouth to protect the wafer from an accidental slip onto the floor and allowed it to absorb into the skin of his saliva-covered tongue. Unexpectedly, the wafer had an odd, acidic taste to it. With a light crunch, he broke the wafer in his mouth and then swallowed its tiny, super thin shards.

"What an odd taste," he thought, as he moved away from the communion area and found an aisle leading out of the church. Outside, it was a beautiful, bright and cool day. Stephen decided to drive over to a local park and just reflect for a while on things in general.

By the time he got to the park, he noticed his stomach was a little upset and that he was developing a bit of a headache. Finding a space at the end of the asphalt lot closest to a small hill overlooking a large duck pond, Stephen parked his 1987 white Ford Bronco and shut off the engine. With a deep breath, he locked the driver's side door and walked into the park.

At the top of the grassy knoll overlooking the dark, brackish green water of the pond, Stephen decided he felt like sitting down for a spell. The grass was dry and soft and he quietly watched several mallards slowly paddling around some cattails at the edge of the pond. A wave of sleepiness slowly worked its way through his consciousness, inexorably overpowering him. Closing his eyes, he gently fell back onto the grass. In seconds he was out cold.

—

When Stephen opened his eyes again, he was standing up, his back against a dusty, hard, rock wall. There was a terrible stench in the air, nearly enough to gag him at first, and he was in the middle of a fair-sized crowd—a crowd apparently waiting on something, or somebody.

At first he couldn't understand what was being said by the throng around him. The people seemed to be speaking in two or three different languages but amazingly, in just a few moments, he began to pick up bits and pieces of conversations. Soon it all became clear. It was a smelly, dirty place, but he could tell what they were saying.

"They will be coming by this way, won't they?" a light-haired man to his left said to another man who stood just inches ahead of them both.

Almost all of the people he could see close by were dark-haired, short, skinny like-they-were-four-meals-away-from-being-full-people, skinny like pictures he'd seen of third world countries in books and magazines. They were dressed in dirty, tattered clothes that were more like filthy blankets tied around their waists with small lengths of rope.

"It's the only way to the killing hill," the light-haired man's companion said.

This fellow was small like the rest of the crowd, with an olive-complexion mostly buried behind layers of dirt and grease and equally greasy and dirty dark hair. The odors were almost more than Stephen could bear again. He slid a couple of feet down the rock wall away from the two men. It was a little better there. "They always pass this way, you must know that by now."

Stephen ventured a glance to the front. Beyond the crowd, which was three to five people deep in most places, he could see a pathway, maybe it was a road, irregularly lined with stones. The road was probably half rock and half just dusty dirt, he estimated, although when he looked off to his left, toward the "killing hill," the road became not much more than a worn-down trail, one rutted with tracks of heavily-laden carts. Squinting into the distance towards the hill, he thought he saw what looked like thick sticks or logs sticking out of the ground there but he couldn't be sure.

To his right was a city. Not a huge city but a busy one. He could see many people moving around the narrow streets closest to where he stood and there were several round-topped buildings that reminded him of middle-eastern temples or synagogues he'd seen in picture books. The people in the crowd around him were looking for something coming from the direction of the city because they kept turning that way and making a kind of clucking noise. Stephen peered that way but could see nothing.

Since no one in the crowd seemed to notice him, he moved around a bit, trying to take in his strange new surroundings with its equally strange people and unexpectedly powerful smells. At the sound of cries coming from off to the right, he slid back into the crowd, back where he had started, next to the two men.

"They must be coming," the light-haired man said.

"These displays disgust me," the second man said boldly.

"Hush," his friend warned him, eyes darting around at the nearby people. "Someone may hear."

"I don't care," the second man said, "they've done nothing but crush us since they came."

"Look." the first man tried to shift the attention off himself and his wildly talking friend. "Here they come."

Because he was a full head taller than those around him, Stephen was able to see over most of the crowd and he could see to the right a small contingent of people working their way up the cobblestone and dirt roadway.

"Can you see him yet?" an old, scraggly-haired woman to his right said to no one in particular. Stephen leaned forward for a better view and the woman suddenly jerked away.

"What is it?" An equally old woman beside her said.

"Lord God," the first old lady said. "I thought I saw something beside me."

"Devils." The second woman cringed. She aimed two fingers of one hand at the spot the first woman indicated. "It's the Devil's day."

To try and avoid anyone else detecting him, Stephen carefully moved back in behind the first two men. One of them turned his head in his direction but didn't seem to take any undue notice.

"They're here," someone shouted. "It's them."

"How many?" Someone else said.

"Four," the first voice said.

Though he didn't really need to, Stephen found himself standing on tiptoes to get a clear view of the oncoming procession. As it passed by, he saw four men, all beaten severely, their backs a bloody, naked mess, being driven up the cobblestone path by a small contingent of soldiers, dressed in classic Roman Legionary uniforms, their short swords at the side and each wielding either a whip or a cudgel-like stick of wood which they used to prod their often reluctantly moving prisoners.

"Which one?" The dark-haired man said. "Which one is the rebel teacher?"

"That's him on the far side," the light-haired man explained. "Beyond the two bigger men on this side."

Stephen looked out to see a rather smallish man, perhaps average-sized among these shorter peoples, with the ubiquitous dark, curly hair—so curly as to almost be in ringlets. The man looked tired, dirty, and not surprisingly, afraid.

"That's Yeshua," the light-haired man said, "that's him."

"They say he had many dangerous men in his band," the dark-haired man opined.

"Oh, yes," his companion agreed.

"Zealots and radicals, even Iscarii," the dark-haired man said.

"Hush," the other man said, "don't even say those names. Not out loud."

"He was a reformer," someone else said. "Nothing more."

"See," the light-haired man hissed to his friend, "they've heard you. Be quiet about it."

"I was just saying," the dark-haired man said.

"Enough," his friend told him, "enough. There they go."

The four condemned men passed by then, followed by a large oxen cart that contained four tall wooden beams cut from tree limbs. As the procession continued up the road to the ominous hill, part of the crowd fell in behind, keeping a safe distance from the whips, cudgels, and swords of the Legionaries. Stephen tagged along, although his movements seemed to be attracting an occasional confused glance from members of the throng.

As the condemned men and the ones in the crowd who followed them neared the killing hill, they were suddenly overtaken by a larger unit of Legionaries who came stomping up from behind, sending the crowd scattering for safety.

"Arrogant bastards," the dark-haired man whispered to his friend when they were safely out of harm's way from the probable Century of Legionaries. The soldiers formed a solid ring around the vertical beams before which the condemned men now stood.

The two men Stephen followed, unseen as he was at their side, had hurried off the path to the left center of the killing hill. Before them were the remains of several men previously sentenced to death. Parts of their decomposing bodies hung from nearby T-shaped vertical and horizontal beams upon which they had died and upon which they still hung.

Mangy dogs, their own ribs sticking from starving sides, poked their heads over the backside of the hill, hoping for a quick bite when the Legionaries didn't bother to drive them off.

"Filthy Romans," the light-haired man whispered.

"Why are there so many of them?" the dark-haired man said.

"Why do you think?"

"The outcountry rabbi?"

"Exactly. They're afraid there'll be trouble."

"There aren't enough people here to scare the animals off." The dark-haired man said. "Much less fight these bloody soldiers."

"Shows how powerful his band had become."

"Hmm."

Before them, the soldiers prepared the four condemned men to hang on the wooden beams. First they did the biggest man among the four, a foul, evil-looking man with one protruding eye that looked dead of sight. They laid him on the ground with his arms on the crossbeam and drove thick hobnails through his hands just up his arm from the wrist. His cry was bloodcurdling and most in the crowd looked away in terror.

Then with a contraption made of rope and pulleys, which they hooked around the man's shoulders and around his waist, the Legionaries drug the man backwards to the vertical beam and then hoisted him, screaming, into place.

Once the crossbeam was nailed and tied solidly to the vertical beam to make a T, a thick-waisted Legionary drove an even thicker hobnail into the man's crossed legs just above the ankles. Again the cry was bloodcurdling. The procedure was repeated on the remaining three men with exactly the same results.

In their final configuration, the four men were not quite in a straight line, the small rebel teacher second in line from the left and slightly back from the others. Finally the Legionaries added a sign for each of the criminals. One bore the inscription, *EP*. Another *FC*. The big man—on the far right of the four—had the label *HV*. And the rebel leader, *YNHC*.

"What are those signs?" the dark-haired man asked.

"Two of them are common thieves or robbers," his friend explained, "the big man is a murderer."

"Ooh," the dark-haired man shivered.

"And the little one—enemy of the state."

Staring at the horrendous display finally took its toll on Stephen. He closed his eyes and drifted away in his mind. It was all too terrible, too real. He wanted to be somewhere else, anywhere else. It was just too much. A wave of nausea swept over him and he had to fight an urge to vomit.

When it passed, he opened his eyes. Oddly, it seemed that several hours had passed. The two talkative men had gone, as well as most of the original crowd. The sun was well below noon height and far in the distance there was a desert thunderstorm blowing wind and rain across the barren land.

Looking up, he saw that the four condemned men were in various stages of dying. Occasionally they would manage to stretch themselves to get a breath of air but it was obvious they were dying of asphyxiation. Then a Legionary, a commander of some rank, signaled to the thick-bodied soldier who had nailed the men to the beams, and the big man stepped towards the condemned men. He wielded a heavy metal bar.

Without a word, the soldier swung the bar at the legs of the big murderer and shattered them at mid-calf range. The man made a muffled groan and slumped heavily downward. In turn, the soldier repeated the procedure on the other three men with, once again, identical results.

In no more than a quarter of an hour, all of the condemned were dead. Stephen looked away from them and at the people remaining on the hill. Only a few were left, including some dark-clothed women nearby. They cried softly. Beyond them, he saw yet another contingent of men arriving. They appeared to be high-ranking officials accompanied by a handful of what were surely priests. They saluted the Legionary commander and he walked them over to the beam holding the rebel teacher. Stephen followed, hoping not to be seen. As he drew nearer the rebel's beam, one of the women looked up and seemed to see him, but she made no indication to the others that she had.

"This is him," the Legionary commander said, pointing up to the little rabbi. "As you can see, he is dead."

"Make sure they are all dead," one of the officials, perhaps a representative of the Governor, ordered. The commander signaled to a lower ranking man who pointed to his men. Several soldiers grabbed spears and pierced the sides of the four already dead men just below the heart on the left side of their bodies. Blood and fluids poured out of the wounds onto the beams and onto the sandy soil below. The starving dogs just off the side of the killing hill howled their hunger.

"Sir?" The commander said, as if there were anything else to be done to the men.

"Your rebellion is over," the Governor's representative said to the priests. "Done."

"Yes," one of the priests said, tight-jawed. "Yes, it is."

With a salute, the Governor's representative and his party turned and walked away. The Legionary commander signaled his unit and the large contingent of soldiers marched off as well. Stephen was left alone with the dead, the dark-clothed ladies, and the original contingent of soldiers.

Nearly dizzy from viewing the harsh brutality of local justice, he wobbled forward, finding himself near to the base of the dead rabbi's beam. He reached out a hand and leaned against the beam. A nearby Legionary swung his head over as if he'd seen something.

"What is it?" One of his comrades, the big soldier who had broken the prisoners' legs, said.

Stephen froze where he stood.

"I thought I saw something move at the base of that beam there," the first Legionary said.

"You're just jittery," the big soldier said. "You're new out here. You'll get used to these little shows."

"I don't know," the first soldier said. "It's rough. I sure wouldn't want to die like this."

"You wouldn't," a third soldier said, as the three troops gathered a few feet away from the beam holding the dead body of the rebel teacher. "Unless you were a traitor. These types of executions are only for non-Romans."

"Oh," the first soldier said, as if relieved.

"It's a message to these barbarians," the big soldier explained. "Rome to the provinces—we're in control. We rule. Our laws. Don't break them."

"What did this man do?" The first soldier pointed at the teacher.

"Who cares," the big soldier said. "These people are goat herders. Desert rats. They're backwards and filthy. In case you haven't noticed yet, this is the worst posting in the entire army. You think anybody wants to be here in this Godforsaken place."

"I don't know," the first soldier said.

"Hell," the big man said, "our governor can't even stand the place. I'm telling you it is the crappiest place in the empire. Horrible."

"Easy on him," the third soldier interjected, "he's new here. Give him some time."

"Hmph," the big soldier grunted.

"To answer your question about this one," the third soldier explained to the first, "he was the leader of some sort of out country rebellion. It was getting out of control. We stopped it."

"Oh," the first soldier said.

He and the third soldier walked away then, the more experienced man putting his arm around the new man's shoulders and explaining to him the facts of life in this occupied land at the furthest edges of the great empire. The big soldier remained by the beam that held the dead body of the radical teacher.

Having been still as long as he could, Stephen could not resist an urge to reach up and touch the dead man above him. The man looked so small, so alone in his death. Stephen felt a great wave of sadness and compassion sweep over him. For the man, for all the men dead on that horrible hill.

Slowly he lifted his right arm towards the beam, towards the large hobnail driven through the dead man's feet. Giving in to a strange impulse, then, he suddenly grabbed for the nail and pulled on it. The big soldier, spying the movement, cried out. Despite that, Stephen kept pulling on the nail. The big soldier bolted towards the beam, grabbing a nearby cudgel. Stephen turned just in time to see the cudgel coming straight at his forehead. Then everything went dark.

—

He woke to the declining sun in his eyes. It was late in the afternoon. The park was completely empty except for him and the ducks swimming around in the pond below.

What a strange thing to have dreamed about. He sat up and tried to clear the cobwebs out of his head. He'd been having several of these lately. They were quite odd.

As he started to stand, he felt something on his shirt near his waist. Looking down he saw that it was a two or three inch strip of some rough-hewn, dark metal. Taking the object in his fingers, he examined it, saw to his shock that it was a thin piece of a nail. A break off, a flake, from one side of a primitive-looking hobnail.

He quickly finished standing, almost jumping up, and looked around for other people in the park, but there were none. Taking a deep breath, he held the nail up to see it better. It looked exactly like a piece of the nail he had touched just before he had blacked out in his dream, just as he was about to touch the nail on the feet of the....

Impossible.

Could not have happened.

Checking around for other people again, he quickly pocketed the nail flake. He took another deep breath to calm himself down, releasing it in an audible, tired, even sad-sounding sigh. Slowly, stiff-legged, he walked down the hill to the parking space and his Bronco. Sliding in behind the wheel he wondered if he dared tell anyone of what seemed to have happened. Lisa? Tom?

The confession priest? Not likely. Oh, no, he wouldn't do that. How could he tell such a story to anyone? How would he be able to tell the priest about the emptiness he felt looking up at the sad little man forever dead on the Roman T beam? His lifeless body no more than a cold husk or shell for the human vitality it had once housed.

No, he would have to keep this one to himself. He would not go back to the church, nor to the priests, and he wouldn't tell Tom or Lisa either. Some experiences were too personal, too individual to share. This was one he would have to keep to himself—to himself alone, forever.

EXILE

"You're coming over to my grandma's house tomorrow night and that's that," Tom Harris decisively told his friend Stephen White.

The two young software engineers were taking a short break in the snack bar just outside the "bullpen" area where their work cubicles were situated at the small startup computer animated graphics company Animatec, located in the little town of Nevada in west central Missouri.

"I don't know."

"Don't pretend you already have plans, I know better. Besides, you love Grandma's glese. We had it before a couple of times, remember? You raved about it."

"Yeah." Stephen recalled that the dish was a kind of large dumpling covered in a creamy, rich, white gravy. "It was good. Great."

"Then it's settled. Want me to pick you up?"

"No, no. I know where your grandma lives."

"Up by Smelter Hill."

"I know, I know. I said I knew where she lives."

"Good. I didn't want you to have an excuse for not showing up."

"Is, uh, uh, Lisa coming?"

"No," Tom gave him a knowing smile, "she has a date with some fancy beau she met from up in KC."

"Oh." Stephen tried not to show his disappointment.

It was an open secret between him and Tom and really among all of the people at Animatec that Stephen had a crush on Lisa. Stephen knew that an overweight dorky nerd like himself had no chance whatsoever with a woman like Lisa but he couldn't help himself.

She had sparkling light green eyes, wavy brown hair, and a tight little bottom and flat tummy from working out all the time to keep herself in shape to the max. All that and the fact that she also had beautiful, full, round breasts—at least that's how they looked in her stylish, tight blouses—all that conspired to make her the object of Stephen's unrequited love.

"Be there about six or so." Tom said. "We'll have a drink or something before we eat. And talk about something other than work—or Lisa Backman."

"Uh-oh, uh, sure." Stephen drug himself back to reality from the mental image he had conjured of Lisa. "Six or so."

"Be there." Tom said. "Or be square."

—

"The glese is almost ready, boys," Tom's grandmother called from the kitchen door. "Is the table all set?"

"Yes, grandma," Tom answered. "I set everything out just like you told me."

"All right, it'll just be another minute or two. You boys can sit at the table if you want."

"What kind of food is glese?" Stephen said to Tom as they stood up from where they had been sitting out in the living room. "I forgot."

"Russian," Tom answered, "some kind of old country meal."

"You mean from Russia Russian?"

"Yeah, grandma's parents came from the Ukraine or somewhere like that."

"How'd she end up in Nevada?"

"I don't know exactly," Tom and Stephen reached the dining room table and stood beside it waiting for grandma, "but when they came to the U.S. they somehow ended up in what they call the South Russian Bottom up in Lincoln, Nebraska. Grandma met Grandpa Barton up there and they got married and moved down here to Nevada. Grandpa worked for years on the railroad."

"I never knew him," Stephen said.

"No. He passed away quite a few years ago."

"I noticed there were a bunch of books on the coffee table by Russian writers. Is she big on that?"

"I think grandpa was. She just left them out like when he was still here."

"I see."

"Okay, boys." Tom's grandmother came out of the kitchen with a tray on which were three big soup bowls full of the creamy glese. "Sit down."

"Smells great, grandma." Tom sniffed the food.

"Looks great, too," Stephen added.

"Everyone has something to drink?" Grandmother Barton said.

"Yes, ma'am." The boys lifted glasses of ice water for inspection.

"Good, now help yourself to some bread, and there's veggies, too. Corn, peas, help yourselves."

"Thank you, grandma." Tom took a slice of thick, dark bread from a nearby platter. Stephen did the same.

From the first bite, Stephen's taste buds were overwhelmed by the extremely rich concoction. Glese had something of the taste of southern biscuits and gravy, relatively bland but with the creamy, buttery richness of a dairy sauce on cooked bread. He could taste salt and pepper in the dish and something else, maybe oregano. Whatever the recipe, the final result was an extremely satisfying meal, albeit one that was so rich it nearly left him lightheaded when he had wolfed it all down.

"Would you like more, Stephen?" Mrs. Barton watched him scrape his bowl with the large spoon he had used for eating.

"No, ma'am. I'm so full, I think I'm going to bust."

"Let us help you clean up, grandma," Tom offered.

"No, no, you boys go on back in the living room and visit some more. I'll take care of all this."

'Thank you, Mrs. Barton," Stephen said. "It was a wonderful meal."

"It was great, grandma," Tom added. "Really."

"Thank you, boys. Now go on. I'll do the cleanup."

Back in the living room, Stephen and Tom sat down on opposite ends of a big, comfortable couch.

Stephen leaned back, took a deep breath and then belched—loudly.

"You okay?" Tom said.

"Yeah, I'm just really full, that's all. That glese is really good but it's really a meal. And super rich."

"Very rich."

After several minutes where the two young men just sat on the couch quietly lost in their own thoughts, Stephen began to feel a little odd. He fidgeted in his seat and belched softly several times. Tom looked over at him.

"You okay, man?"

"I don't know. I'm feeling lightheaded all of a sudden. Kind of dizzy. Kind of tired."

"Here, here," Tom stood up, "I'll sit on the recliner. You stretch out for a minute. Maybe you just need a quick nap or something."

Tom stayed by the couch until Stephen put his feet up on it, then he sat down in the recliner.

"Is something wrong, Tommy?" Grandma Barton came into the room drying her hands with a kitchen towel.

"Stephen's feeling a little woozy, grandma," Tom explained. "I think maybe he overate."

"Oh, dear, I feel terrible. Let me get him a bicarbonate, maybe that will help."

"It's okay, Mrs. Barton," Stephen said weakly, "I'm just feeling a little tired."

In fact, Stephen was feeling weak. He could feel the energy ebbing from his body like a slowly withdrawing tide. His eyelids grew heavy and he closed them just to rest a moment. As he drifted off, he could hear Tom and Grandma Barton fussing over him but he was too tired to reassure them or to stop himself from fading out.

A moment later, he drifted completely off.

—

When Stephen opened his eyes, at first he couldn't tell where he was. It was cold and damp and the light was poor. In a few moments he began to make out the surroundings. It was definitely not Grandma Barton's living room and he was not lying on her couch. In fact, he was sitting up on a small bed or cot. The smelly mattress seemed to be made of straw or something because it made a scrunching sound when he moved around on it.

The room itself was rectangular, maybe twenty feet long and eight to ten wide. There was a window high up to his left but it appeared to be covered with something that blocked most of the outside illumination.

Up high on the opposite wall was some kind of artificial light source that sputtered and spewed and did little else. Stephen couldn't tell if it was a lamp or some odd kind of candle. To the back left was a rudimentary sink and toilet and a bare table. Directly across from him was an empty chair. To his right from the chair was a big wooden door with metal hinges and locks.

"This is a jail," he said out loud to the empty room. "I'm in a cell. I'm in prison. What the...."

Just as he was about to leap up and start crying out for help, a rattling at the door stopped him cold.

"Oh, Lord," he whispered, "somebody's coming."

Stephen curled up on one end of the bed and tried to make himself small and hopefully unseen. After the clanking of heavy keys, the door swung open and a tall, emaciated, wild-bearded man with equally wild eyes and a shock of unkempt hair was pushed into the room by what looked like a military guard. Stephen cringed in his seat, but the guard didn't seem to notice him.

After exchanging words in some language Stephen didn't know but thought might be East European of some sort, the guard left the bearded man in the room and walked back out to the corridor beyond the cell. The guard slammed the door shut, causing a terrifying clang, and then locked it from the outside.

As the echo of the slammed door faded, the tall man walked to the toilet facilities and, after groaning and moaning several times, came back and sat down in the chair directly across the room from Stephen. The man put his head in his hands and wept softly, quietly to himself.

After a full moment, in which Stephen held his breath for fear of being heard and thereby possibly seen, the man looked up—directly at Stephen. Stephen stared back at the man intently. Slowly, the man pulled back in his chair, a surprised look on his face.

"Oh, God," Stephen exhaled.

"Aha!" the man exclaimed, causing Stephen to nearly leap up from his seat on the bed. "Aha! There you are."

"W… what?" Stephen gritted his teeth. "You can see me?"

"Why wouldn't I see you?" the man declared. "I'm looking right at you."

"I didn't know you would be able to see me." Stephen didn't really comprehend what was happening or what he himself was even talking about, nor how or why he was now able to understand the man's language and apparently speak it.

"I sensed you were there," the man said directly to him. "You've been hiding from me, haven't you?"

"No I haven't. I just got here."

"I knew you were there."

"Where? Where am I?"

"It's all right," the man told him. "What does it matter? You're here now. At last."

"At last?"

"Yes." The look of near-madness in the man's eyes caused Stephen to involuntarily recoil.

"W...who, who do you think I am?"

"Who are you indeed? What is your name?"

"Stephen."

"Stefan." The man instantly converted Stephen's name into his language.

"Yes, I guess."

"What is your father's name?"

"My father?"

"Your father."

"Uh, his name is, uh, David."

"Stefan Davidovich." The man extended a raw, bony hand to Stephen. "Good to know you."

"Who are you?" Stephen shook the man's cold, clammy hand.

"Who am I?" the man made something like a laughing sound. "What a question. I am Nikolai Pavlovich Grigoriev. How can you not know that when I have been expecting you for so long?"

"Where are we?"

"You are strangely uninformed, Stefan Davidovich, especially for a guardian spirit."

"You think I'm your guardian spirit?"

"Of course. What else could you be?"

"Where are we?" Stephen tried again.

Obviously," Grigoriev explained as if to a child, "this is the famous and infamous Peter-and-Paul fortress. The Tsar's personally built prison."

"Then... then," Stephen began, "we are ...."

"Prisoners. Criminals. The worst kind. Enemies of the state. We committed the crime of free-thinking. Oh, yes, that was our crime. We talked like children, each week at Petrashevski's. We blathered on about Fourier, Socialism, Pushkin. Terrible criminals we are."

"How long have you been here? In this jail?"

"Since the spring."

"It's winter now?"

"Yes. It is winter."

"And only for ..." Stephen started, but was stopped by the man's long-fingered, uplifted hand."

"Shh. I hear something."

Stephen listened intently. There was the sound of boots in the outside corridor. Of cells being opened. Of people speaking.

"Oh, my Lord." Grigoriev wrung his hands. "They are coming back. They've come for us."

"Come for us?"

The cell door was unlocked again and seconds later it swung widely open.

"Nikolai Pavlovich Grigoriev," the same military guard who had brought the prisoner in before said expressionless, tossing a handful of what was obviously warm weather clothing at the man, "put these on immediately and follow me."

—

It was bone-chillingly cold in St. Petersburg's Semenovsky Square when the carriages bringing the prisoners arrived there just at sunrise. Blanketed by almost a foot of snow, it would have been a beautiful sight were it not for the huge, imposing scaffolding, with black crepe hung all around, set in its center.

The prisoners, at first chatting with each other as much as their guards would allow, were shortly silenced by military officials who corralled the men at the base of the scaffolding, which was ringed completely by armed soldiers. No one could miss seeing several stakes driven into the ground at the side of the scaffolding, stakes unmistakably used for firing squads.

Stephen stood behind Grigoriev in one of two prisoner lines the guards had ordered. It was all too strange for him. He could feel the cold, the wetness of the snow, the horrible tension among the prisoners—and yet no one but Grigoriev seemed to pay any attention to him. Listening intently, he caught several threads of conversation among the highly agitated prisoners.

"They are going to shoot us," someone behind Stephen said.

"Hush," another man said. "They can do no such thing."

"I don't believe," the first man said, "that I have ever thought more clearly than at this moment."

"You'll no doubt turn it into a story, ey, Fedya?" a man in front of Grigoriev called back.

"Who are these men?" Stephen whispered.

"The tall, confident man at the front of us," Grigoriev replied, "is Petrashevski himself. It was his little study circles that brought us to this point. The man directly before me is Speshnev, the most radical of all."

"What are you mumbling about, Nikolai Pavlovich?" Speshnev turned towards Grigoriev angrily. "Have you gone mad?"

"It would not be so strange, would it," the one called Fedya said. "Eight months of boredom, isolation, filth. Could anyone stay sane?"

"Feodor Mikhailovich," Grigoriev explained quietly to Stephen, "is a great writer. He is the most famous, and talented, of us all."

"Stop jabbering, Grigoriev," Speshnev said.

"Oh." Grigoriev snickered like a child.

At that moment there was a sudden commotion. A high-ranking officer in a cape rode up on a dark, lathered horse. A soldier ran to hold the reins as the man dismounted.

"A general," Grigoriev told Stephen.

"Shut up," Speshnev growled.

As the newly-arrived officer prepared to make some sort of pronouncement, Stephen managed a quick look at the other prisoners. He counted some twenty of them. All wore old-fashioned clothes far too light for the freezing, heavy snow conditions. Stephen shivered, wondered again at the peculiar situation he found himself in.

"Quiet." The voice of the general burst into Stephen's icy reverie. "The prisoners will be silent. At once. Be still!"

Conversation among the prisoners ceased. The general walked back and forth before them, swinging a riding crop by his side. He seemed to be impatiently awaiting something. The prisoners watched his every step.

Shortly, another official arrived in the square. This time he was a civilian, however, but he carried several documents with him and had an air of authority that was even more pronounced than that of the general.

Reading from the documents, he called each prisoner by name and ordered them to line up in the sequence their names were read, Petrashevski and Speshnev at the head, with Grigoriev in back. Stephen, positioning himself behind Grigoriev, prayed fervently that no one else could see him and that his name, however improbable it might be, would not be among those read.

Finally, a priest came up, holding a large cross. He intoned a prayer for the prisoners then walked towards the stairs leading up onto the scaffolding. The prisoners understood to follow.

Up on the scaffolding, the prisoners were divided into two groups, again with Petrashevski, Speshnev, and the unstable Grigoriev at the head of the first group. Stephen continued to hide behind Grigoriev and two men behind them was the writer called Feodor Mikhailovich, or Fedya. Shortly, the civilian official cleared his throat and began reading the prisoners' sentences. They were all the same and the official stopped before each prisoner and read quickly, almost unintelligibly from his papers.

"The law has condemned you to death by firing squad," he repeated some twenty times, only the first few times drawing any reaction from the growing crowd below the scaffolding, "and the Tsar has given his confirmation of the sentence."

"They cannot mean to execute us," the writer, Fedya, said to the man directly behind Stephen. "Can they, Durov?"

Durov simply pointed at a cart beside the scaffolding that was covered in straw matting.

"Dear Jesu," Fedya moaned, "coffins. God cannot mean to do this to us."

"God has little to do with this, my friend," Durov told Fedya.

"Hush, you men." The priest came up to the front of the prisoners. The men hung their heads. "Brothers," the priest went on, "before your death you must repent. Repent in the name of Jesus Christ. Confess. Repent."

"Repent, hell." Speshnev spat at the priest.

"God forgives you, brother."

But when the priest moved among the condemned men, nearly all kissed the cross, even virulent Speshnev and stoic Petrashevski—the staunchest atheists among the condemned, Grigoriev explained softly to Stephen.

Suddenly, guards appeared and grabbed the first three men from the first line, Petrashevski, Speshnev, and Grigoriev, Stephen attempting to hide in the folds of the gaunt man's worn and tattered clothing, and drug them down off the scaffolding and tied them to the stakes on the ground. Durov and Fedya saw that they would be next in line.

"Lord help us," Fedya staggered against the wooden rail of the scaffolding.

Down below, a squad of young soldiers, rifles in hand, stood before the men tied to the stakes. They raised the weapons and aimed them at the staked out prisoners, who stood without blindfolds but wore hats to cover their heads from the cold air.

"Goodbye, Speshnev," Petrashevski said calmly.

"And you," Speshnev managed to reply.

"Can't you save us?" Grigoriev demanded of Stephen, turning his head to look directly at his panic-stricken "guardian angel." "You must save us. Please, Lord, help me. I don't want to die. Stefan Davidovich you must find a way. Please."

"Grigoriev's gone mad," Speshnev said to Petrashevski.

"A good place to be now," Petrashevsy replied. "Poor Nikolai Pavlovich."

Grigoriev continued to loudly entreat Stephen, moaning and groaning and talking wildly.

"Shut him up," the old general yelled at a young soldier in the firing squad.

The young soldier broke ranks and came up to Grigoriev. "Please be quiet, sir. You're upsetting everyone."

Grigoriev continued to jabber, but quieter. He turned once more to Stephen, begging him to save them both, to help him escape.

The young soldier, feeling the hair stand up on the back of his neck, looked past Grigoriev as if their might be someone there the madman was speaking to. For just a moment, the boy thought he did see something just beyond the big prisoner.

With a small yelp, the young soldier leapt back from Grigoriev, turned and hurried back to his squad.

"What was it?" One of his mates said.

"Nothing," the young soldier said, unable to take his eyes off the area around the madman. "Nothing. I didn't see anything."

"Attention!" the general called to the firing squad. The staked out prisoners waited for the end. "Present arms!" An involuntary groan escaped the lips of most of the condemned.

Suddenly, a rider dashed into the square, waving papers in one hand. The civilian official walked over and joined the general by the firing squad. The two men looked at each other solemnly. Then came the roll of drums, beating the sound of retreat.

"Dear God," Fedya cried from the scaffolding. "We're saved."

The rider dismounted and addressed the general.

"His Worship, the Tsar," the man announced, "in the kindness of his great soul, has commuted the death sentence of these men. Here are the new sentences." He handed the papers he carried to the general.

"Very well," the general said magnanimously, "release the men at the stakes."

On the scaffolding there was a great wave of joy, followed by tears and the near collapse of many of the prisoners. On the ground, the men at the stakes were released. Guards helped them back towards the scaffolding.

As they walked back, Speshnev had to be supported on either side by soldiers and even Petrashevski, attempting defiance to the last, stumbled as he got to the stairs leading back up to the scaffold. But Grigoriev was inconsolable. He could not bear up.

"Why did you not help me?" he repeated to Stephen. "How could you desert me, Stefan Davidovich? How could you?"

"I'm not who you think I am," Stephen tried hard to stay behind Grigoriev and in his shadow. "I don't even know what's happening. I'm sorry. I would help you if I could."

"He's gone completely mad," the general commented. "Utterly insane."

"Too late, the Tsar's reprieve," the civilian official couldn't hide a smile, "ey?"

"The general laughed, with little humor. "From death to exile."

"Look out, sir," the young soldier who had attempted to quiet Grigoriev suddenly cried out. "Look out beside the madman."

"Oh, hell." Stephen made eye contact with the young soldier. "Son of a …."

"What is it?" the general said.

The young soldier sprung forward with his rifle raised, butt first. He aimed squarely at Stephen's forehead and jabbed forward with all his might.

"Damn it." Stephen tried to grab onto Grigoriev's ragged shirt, "I don't …."

—

Stephen felt someone patting his cheeks softly with something cool and soft. His head hurt and he was reluctant to open his eyes. There was a bright, painful light on the other side of his eyelids. Finally, after another moment or so, the pain began to subside and the light dimmed. Stephen slowly opened his eyes, fearful of where he might find himself.

"Stephen." Grandma Barton leaned over him, "Stephen, are you all right?"

"Oh, thank God." Stephen closed his eyes again and took a deep breath.

At least he knew where he was again. He was back home, back in his own town, not in some frozen Russian square surrounded by prisoners facing firing squads. Yes, he was starting to feel much better. When he ventured to look at the world again, he saw Tom Harris staring down at him from behind Grandma Barton.

"Are you okay, buddy?"

"How long was I out?"

"Just a few minutes."

"Really? My God, it seemed like a long time."

"We were getting ready to call the paramedics, young man," Grandma Barton interjected.

"I'm sorry."

"Let me go run some more cold water on this cloth. You just stay there on the couch. I'll be right back."

"You're looking better," Tom said, when his grandma had left the room. "We were worried about you there for a minute."

"I was worried about me, too." Stephen slowly pulled himself up to a sitting position.

"What happened?"

"Man, I don't know. I was gone."

"Gone? What do you mean? Where gone?"

"I was in another place," Stephen tried to explain, "I was like in Russia or something, a long time ago."

"Russia?" Tom said. "I'm not gonna let you eat Grandma's glese again."

"Sounds crazy, doesn't it?" Stephen admitted, shaking his sore head.

He leaned back on the couch and stretched, reached his hands behind his head.

"That's funny." He pulled his right hand back to where he could see it.

"What is?"

Stephen looked down at his right hand. Between the index and middle fingers was a piece of ragged, off-white, coarse cloth—just as mad Grigoriev had worn.

"It can't be."

"Can't be?" Tom said. "Can't be what. What did you say?"

Stephen rubbed the cloth in his fingers, held it to his nose, smelled its pungent odor. Saw the terrible, cold square again, the frightened, emaciated men.

"What do you have there, Stephen?"

"It's nothing." Stephen pocketed the cloth. "Nothing at all."

"I don't understand." Tom tilted his head at Stephen.

"Neither do I," Stephen said truthfully, "neither do I."

HUMIDIFIER

Stephen felt sick. His head hurt, he coughed frequently, and his sinuses were producing volumes of mucus that steadily drained down into his stomach making him feel nauseated. He had enough of a fever to feel alternately hot and cold. He moaned loudly and belched.

"I'm sick," he said to his living room, where he had ensconced himself uncomfortably on his small couch so that he could at least watch TV, even though that was hardly worth the effort during the day. It only took about two minutes of the soaps and talk shows to convince you that American civilization was regressing by the second and at a frighteningly exponential rate.

"TV sucks," Stephen added to the empty room. "It's crap. And no one knows I'm sick or even cares. I wish somebody was here to take care of me for a change."

Just as Stephen finished his pathetic whine, there was a knock on the door. The sound startled him, scared him a little bit even, for he had been far into self-pity and the sound coming so close to his audible plea for help made him think that maybe someone or something was watching over or looking at him all the time. It made him more than a little paranoid.

"Who is it?" He coughed weakly. "I'm sick."

"Stephen." He heard a familiar, to him angelic, voice call. "Open up. It's me, Lisa."

"Oh, my God." he groaned. All he could think of was that if Lisa came into his crappy little apartment she might see what a slug he really was, how dirty his place was, that his underwear…. "Just a minute," he croaked, trying to get out of bed.

"Stephen."

"Ah, hell," he muttered, too sick to even care about the woman he most admired in the whole world, the one he wished he was cool enough to even dare to ask out, seeing his dirty clothes or his stinky, filthy underwear. "It's open. Come in."

Lisa bustled into the room, arms loaded with foodstuffs and medicines for colds and the flu. She had a quart carton of pure orange juice, a squirt bottle of throat spray, aspirin, cold tablets, a thermos of chicken soup, and a small loaf of homemade, uncut bread. To Stephen she was Florence Nightingale and Rachel Ray rolled up into one beautiful package.

"How did you know I was sick?" He couldn't believe his good luck. Maybe going to confession and to mass recently was paying off after all.

"Work, silly." Lisa put the medicines on an end table near the couch and then pulled the table up close to Stephen.

"Oh, sure." He momentarily suppressed a cough. "Tom, I suppose."

"You sound terrible. Have you taken anything?"

"I had an ibuprofen."

"For heaven's sakes." Lisa said. "That's terrible."

"I know, I know." Stephen attempted a forlorn look at his beautiful and compassionate co-worker. She had never looked more lovely, nor seemed sweeter to him than at this moment.

"I'm going to pour you some of this chicken soup I brought and cut you a little bread. There's some OJ for vitamin C and then you're going to take some cold and flu pills and before you know it you'll feel all good again."

"You're so wonder…" Stephen checked himself at the sudden absence of that trademark beautiful smile on Lisa's full, lovely lips. "I mean, you're a real friend. I mean it."

"I mean, I mean," she teased him. "You must work in the Department of Redundancy Department."

Stephen tried to laugh but it just made him cough again.

"Take it easy," Lisa told him, "I'll get the chicken soup."

A quarter of an hour later, full of chicken soup and homemade bread, with a cold pill working on his sinuses and fever and the burning itch in his throat temporarily eased, Stephen felt warm and full and sleepy. As he began to drift off, Lisa's face appeared in the fuzzy haze above his head.

"Is that a humidifier over there in the corner, Stephen?" she said. He answered her with a small, odorous burp. "I'll go check."

Stephen turned his head to watch Lisa as she walked across the room to the humidifier his parents had given him for his last birthday present and which he almost never used. It was supposed to help him breathe better but he had never noticed much difference whether it was on or off.

"Can I put the water in this pitcher into it?" Lisa called over.

He stretched his neck some more and saw the pitcher. It was a pitcher of water he'd brought back from an open cave he'd explored a little bit up on the bluffs outside of Nevada along the Marais des Cygnes River. He didn't think it would be good to put it in the humidifier but when he tried to motion to Lisa and tell her not to, his body and voice deserted him.

"Mffnum," was the only sound he was able to muster.

"I'll just pour a little into it."

"Iffnab."

"There, that's enough. Now I'll just turn it on and let you get some rest."

"Wuffda." At least that was close to an old Scandinavian expression Stephen actually knew.

Lisa walked back to the couch and looked down at him. In his glazed-over world, she appeared to have a halo not just around her head but around her entire gorgeous body. He feebly held out a hand but she just smiled and began to rummage through a messy pile of books and magazines on the coffee table.

"Are you reading this?" She held up a large, picture-style book. "*Ruins and Treasures of Mexico and the Caribbean.* Good?"

"Umphh."

"I'm sorry. You're too tired for jabbering aren't you?"

"Ahhch."

"I'm going to clean up a little before I go." Lisa set the book down. "You just go on to sleep. It'll be good for you."

Stephen took a deep breath, felt his body relax, felt himself drifting further off. The air from the humidifier continued spreading around the room, moist and soothing when it first entered his burnt out sinuses. But there was something else in it, too, a funny sort of sharp sensation as well, as if tiny little sparks of molecule-level electricity were sparking against the inner walls of his nose. The sensation continued, strengthened, grew. As he dropped into unconsciousness, he felt the sparks spreading from his nose to his sinuses and then into his brain, everywhere in his body. All over.

Then he was out.

—

"Are you feeling all right?" he heard a familiar voice say. Opening his eyes, he saw Lisa looking right at him.

"Whoa," he exclaimed, looking around.

They were on a street corner in some place Stephen did not recognize. Cars were everywhere on the streets, their drivers apparently trying to set a Guinness Book of World Records for honking. The sidewalks were filled with people hurrying by.

"What's the matter?"

"Where are we?"

"What are you talking about? We're in Rio Piedras."

"Rio Piedras?"

"You know, San Juan. The *Mercado*. The university. Our apartment over in the *finca*."

"Our apartment?"

"Jeez, Stephen, you really are getting sick."

"I'm all right." He took another long look at his strange surroundings. What was he doing here, and with Lisa? She seemed so protective, as if she really cared about him.

"You don't look good to me," she said.

"Really, Lisa, I'm okay. Don't worry."

He took a deep breath and coughed. She gave him a cross look. He stared past her to the busy streets of Rio Piedras. What the hell?

"I have to mail this letter back to your mom and dad," she answered as if on cue. Stephen looked at the letter. The return address said *Stephen and Lisa White.*

"We're married?" he blurted out.

"Good heavens, Stephen, you must have a terrible fever."

"I guess so," he mumbled.

They stopped in front of a small post office kiosk. Stephen recoiled from the reflections in the windows of the little store. Lisa looked like she always did, trim and muscular. But he, Stephen, was trim, too. He wasn't lumpy and out of shape. Something was really weird. He didn't know what was happening.

"What's happening?" he said out loud.

"We're going to mail this letter right here at this post office and then we're going home and I'm putting you to bed."

"Yeah." Stephen felt odd as they entered the building. "Home."

"Diez sellos de aereo," Lisa told the clerk, after shaking her head at Stephen again. "Ten air mail stamps."

"Uno, setenta," the clerk took the stamps out of a drawer behind the window and tossed them on the counter. Lisa dug in her purse for the money.

"Stephen, do you have a dollar? I only have one and I don't want to break a ten for this." He reached into the front pocket of his jeans, well-worn he noted, and pulled out a dollar. Lisa laid the two dollars on the counter. *"Gracia."*

The bored clerk handed back the change. *"Bueno."*

"You're definitely getting sick," Lisa announced when they were outside. "You need to be in bed."

"I feel fine," Stephen lied, back and legs aching.

"We're going home, now. You're going straight to bed."

—

On the walk back to the home Lisa had referred to, they passed a small vendor's pushcart on the street.

"Want a peeled orange?" She pointed to the cart.

The old vendor grinned, exposing a row of teeth with several missing. His face was weather-beaten and dark brown. Stephen imagined there must be dozens of push cart merchants like this man all over Rio Piedras, hundreds more, at least, in the greater San Juan area and who knew how many spread throughout the island. He nodded to the old vendor and wondered how he could know such things about this place.

"I don't think so," he answered.

"You're sick as hell, I can always tell. Don't try to hide it from me."

"My lower back and butt kind of hurt," he conceded. "But I'm not sick yet. It'll probably pass. Maybe I'll shake this off before it gets started. Sometimes it happens."

"*Algo mas, señor?*" The little vendor addressed Stephen, who dallied before the man's cart. he understood the man—why, he didn't know.

"*Si, chocolate.*" He pronounced chocolate like someone who knew a little Spanish—choko-latte.

The vendor produced a small package of plain chocolate. The package had a picture of a Spanish fort on it and the words *El Morro*. Stephen paid the man with change and pocketed the candy. The man saluted the couple as they went on their way.

"Let's leave the *rejas* open," Lisa said about ten minutes later, as they slid back the wrought iron gate that secured the three-sided outdoor room of what he realized was apparently their apartment.

Stephen wobbled across the room and slumped down on a couch, his head resting on a fat, soft pillow. He tiredly watched lizards run in and out of the apartment and smelled the heated freshness of the tropical day. He could tell he was really getting sick because he felt the fever coming on and because his lower back and upper buttocks now ached all the time. That was a sure sign with him. He closed his eyes and tried to rest.

"I can't believe how fast this came on you." Lisa walked over to his side.

"Yeah."

"You're really getting sick now, aren't you?" She touched his brow with her forearm. He felt her soft arm, warm and tender to the touch, felt the heartbeat in her strong pulse. "You wouldn't be lying down like that. Not unless you're really sick. I'm going to take you to the doctor right away."

"No." He reached familiarly for her arm. "It'll be all right. It's just some bug or something. New *gringos* probably have to get it to fit in, you know?"

He tried a little laugh.

"That's dumb," she said. "Why don't you lie still? Are you cold? Here, I'll get you a blanket."

"It's from the Spanish," he told her when she returned with a light blanket and spread it over him. "They brought all these diseases with them."

"Forget the Spaniards. Rest. Lie there. Be quiet. I have to let the cat out, she's going crazy in the house."

When she opened the door, a large tabby rushed out. It ran straight for the backyard in hot pursuit of lizards. He heard the cat sliding across the tile floor but took little pleasure in its exuberance. He closed his eyes.

"Damn," he heard Lisa curse sometime later. "How am I supposed to read this stupid thermometer? It's in centigrade." Stephen didn't even realize she had put the instrument in his mouth. But now he could tell she was scribbling something on a pad. "It's over 100 degrees, I think. Damn it."

"What?" he mumbled, making a half-hearted attempt to turn towards her.

It was evening already and he knew he hadn't moved since the early afternoon. He was so sick he no longer wondered about his peculiar new life. If he was living somewhere in the islands and he was married to Lisa—what the hell? That was a good deal as far as he was concerned.

"The heck with it." Lisa pushed away the pad and pencil.

She went over to the sink and ran cold water over a washcloth. She brought the cool cloth to him and replaced the one already drying on his hot brow.

"Do you love me?" he impulsively blurted out. "Really love me?"

"Of course I do, silly. Why would I worry about you like I do if I didn't?"

"Oh."

"Would you like some water or orange juice?" She pushed Stephen's hair back off his forehead.

"No." His voice was weak and sounded to him like it came from far inside a cave. "No thanks."

"You need liquids," she insisted. "How about a little water?"

"Okay." He touched her hand. She gave him a drink. "Thanks," he slurred, eyes drooping.

Lisa set the water glass down. She rubbed his forehead and into his hair with the cool cloth. He muttered something else, then immediately drifted off to sleep. She lay down beside him.

For a couple of days, Stephen's condition remained the same. At some point, Lisa managed to get him to a doctor, but the man said nothing could be done. It was *La Monga,* the doctor told her, everybody gets it here. It hits gringos especially hard, he joked pleasantly, particularly new residents. He recommended bed rest, aspirin, and lots of liquids. Lisa drug him back home and put him to bed again. There was nothing to do but ride it out.

Lying in bed alone, with Lisa elsewhere for the moment, Stephen felt unbelievably hot, the fever burning everywhere within him like hot coals. After a while he noticed that shadows and shapes on the walls and ceiling had begun to assume patterns. He watched them weave back and forth, take on the form of animals, people, demons. They looked down at him, stared at him, mocked him. He was not disturbed by it—it at least took his mind off the pain and fever. Sometime shortly before dawn, at long last, he drifted off to sleep.

—

His armor clanked and banged against itself and nearly swamped him in the soft sand of the shallow water but he managed to keep up with the others as they struggled ashore. The natives on the island ran wildly towards them throwing warped cane spears and shooting sharpened cane arrows, then ran wildly back. Mostly the projectiles fell ineffectually on the shore or bounced off the armor, but one arrow had found its mark, piercing the throat of the man next to him who fell to the beach, a death gurgle on his lips.

The braver of the natives charged again only to be shot down by thunderous blunderbusses or sliced to pieces by razor-sharp swords. The battle ended quickly. The natives were slaughtered. The beach was red with their blood.

He moved through the village then, taking trinkets, searching for gold. Finding a woman. He had her there in her hut, in front of her old mother, on the ground, without taking off his pants.

They worked the rest of the surviving men from sunup to sundown building forts, carrying supplies, raising crops. The natives were like sullen pets: obedient, hard-working, yours to do with what you will.

He found the woman again. And took her again. As often as he wanted— which was often. He came to live in her hut, with her old mother. And her old mother fed him and gave him fish and meal and a salty soup that he drank and it had a bitter taste and his head began to hurt and his body to ache and he closed his eyes and lay on the beach and he was hot, so hot, unimaginably hot and then it began to rain.

It rained on him there on the beach and everyone was gone and it kept raining and raining and he was cold and soaked and yet it rained still and he was wet and tired. And then he slept and the beach was gone, and the people were gone, and the old woman and the daughter were gone and he was alone, tired, resting, soaked to the bone.

—

Stephen woke to sunlight, surprised to find his head clear, but the bedding was soaked completely through and his body was wet and cold, his clammy hair matted against his head like a dirty mop. He tried to find a dry spot to huddle in but couldn't.

"Lisa. Lisa!" He had to call her several times before she stirred.

"What?" She entered the bedroom. Her voice was still hoarse from sleep. "You okay?"

"I think it broke," he said feebly. "I'm soakin' wet."

"Oh, thank God." She helped him sit up, began pulling off the covers. "You were terrible this time. Here, can you scoot over a little? These things are just drenched."

"He sighed. "I thought I'd had it. I didn't hardly sleep at all last night."

"Sounds like a song to me." Lisa suddenly felt playful. He essayed a weak smile.

She pulled the wet, musty sheets off the bed and tossed them on the floor. She got another set from the chest of drawers. Stephen lay back on the bare mattress.

"I had the most peculiar dream."

"What about?" Lisa unfolded a sheet.

"I'm not sure. Something about Spaniards and natives. *Conquistador* stuff. There was a woman."

"A woman?"

"A beautiful Indian woman. She gave me something that made me sick."

"Good Lord." Lisa said. "You dream about women even when you're down with the flu. What is it with men, anyway?"

"But it was strange, like I was part of all that back then somehow."

"It was just the fever, honey." Lisa moved Stephen over to smooth out a wrinkle in the sheet.

"Yeah, the fever."

"You need to clean up. Are you hungry?"

"No."

"You haven't eaten in days."

"I know."

"The kitty and I were worried about you, you know?"

"I know."

"You scared us to death."

"I'm sorry."

"Sit up again." She tucked in a sheet.

When she was finished she laid him back down. Except for the wet hair and a little chill he felt much better now. Weak but definitely better, definitely well.

"We're not like the damn *conquistadors*, are we, Lisa? I mean invaders and all down here."

"We're students."

"Maybe this flu is some sort of initiation or penance for being intruders coming here."

"Maybe it was just the flu. You've been out of your head."

"Yeah, I suppose."

"You just need to rest, you'll be all right."

"Wish we had a tub."

"I'll help you in the shower."

"Did the cat miss me?"

"Don't you remember?"

"Sort of."

"She was checking on you. Cats sense when you're really sick, you know?"

"Yeah?"

"Of course." She said. "You ought to know that by now."

"I been sick," he said.

"You were really sick."

"Yes." He agreed.

His legs ached but he felt safe. He was again sleepy. Lisa went into the bathroom and brought back a large bath towel. She dried his hair, rubbing some warmth into his body, and helped him into new underclothes.

"You can take a shower later," she said, as he drifted back into a restful sleep, his mouth partly open and emitting erratic snoring-like sounds, "when you're stronger."

"Some flu." Lisa went out onto the patio to feed the cat. "If this is what you have to do to belong here, maybe it isn't worth it. I sure as heck don't want it. I never invaded anywhere."

She took a can of cat food from the counter by the refrigerator, opened it and spooned out some on a dish. The cat hurried over and ate hungrily, making small sounds in the back of its throat.

Outside it was blue and warming, a typical day in the tropics. Lisa stretched and yawned. She went to the refrigerator and took out a carton of milk. A bowl of cereal sounded good to her right then. Stephen lay inside in the house, sleeping comfortably. She rubbed the back of her neck with her left hand and sighed deeply. They had gotten past this one. La Monga was over.

—

Stephen woke knowing that he had been speaking just as he regained consciousness. He opened his eyes slowly, afraid of what he might see or where he might be. He was relieved to see that he was in his apartment and that his fever had broken. He felt tired, more than a little wet and uncomfortable in his rather soggy clothes, but he could tell that he had beaten the flu.

"What strange dreams," he said out loud.

"You were dreaming?" Lisa's voice nearly caused him to jump out of his skin.

"My, God, you're still here?"

"Of course, I've only been here a little while."

"Really? It's only been a little while?"

"Maybe a half-hour. Do you feel better now?"

"I do, but I'm still really tired."

"Take another nap," Lisa said. "Maybe you'll feel even better then."

"Maybe I will." Stephen felt his eyelids getting heavy again. Sleep came fast once more. He let it come. He was too tired to resist.

—

Stephen and Lisa made a quick stop at the visitor's center and then walked across the wide Avenue of the Dead. Down to their left the road ran towards the massive Pyramid of the Sun, located on the right side of the Avenue about halfway down to the Pyramid of the Moon, itself situated at the far end of the archaeological zone.

Climbing up, over, and down a set of steps leading to a wide field called the Ciudadela, featuring a series of low, symmetrically placed stone pyramid platforms, they walked toward the newer and older temples of Queztalcoatl, which were at the back of the expansive Ciudadela. Barely ten yards beyond the steps, the first of the never ending stream of souvenir and trinket vendors approached them.

"*Obsidiana, cuartzo.*" The first vendor described the black rock and clear glass objects he held up for their appraisal. "*Barato*, cheap. Good deal."

"*No, gracias, no.*" Stephen fended the vendor away from them.

He put his arm lightly on Lisa's waist to guide her to the right toward the pyramid of Quetzalcoatl. As they walked, he stopping vendors with a wave or a few words, she drank in the physical environment of the *Ciudadela*—not yet looking to their left towards the majesty of the Pyramid of the Sun or beyond to the slightly lesser presence of the Pyramid of the Moon. He kept up a running monologue while she walked on happily, maybe hearing him, maybe too interested in the reality of the ruins to concentrate on a verbal summary of their history.

"This first one," he pointed to the large pyramid at the back, right center of the *Ciudadela*, "was built on top of the old one. They didn't discover it until they were restoring the front one. The old one is the really interesting one." He pointed up ahead to their right. "It's behind here."

"Great." She put her arm through his. "How do you know so much about it?"

"I must've read it somewhere." Truth was, he didn't really know himself.

Next he led them on around the first pyramid, which they decided not to climb so they could go straight on to the old one.

"Oh, my gosh," Lisa said as soon as the sculpture and architecture of the interior temple could be seen from the walkway that ran between the backside of the newer pyramid and the front of the old. "This is amazing."

She hurried on ahead, stopping directly in front of the partially restored steps that had led in the vastly distant past to the top of the old pyramid where strange rituals had been performed. Rituals only incompletely remembered through archaeological and historical speculation and in the blood running in the veins of Mexico's remaining indigenous population.

"What are these heads?" She pointed to an alternating pattern of sculpted figures running horizontally with each level of steps and vertically at the sides of the steps themselves.

"The ones with the circle eyes," Stephen said, "are *Tlaloc,* the water or rain god. The snake heads are *Quetzalcoatl.* He's the Number One god. The plumed serpent. *La serpienta enplumada.*"

"La serpienta enplumada. What a beautiful name."

"You should hear a native say it. I can't do it justice. It's a beautiful name."

They admired the old temple for several minutes more, moving back and forth on the walkway to get different angles on the ancient ruin. He watched her with his own admiration.

She wore dark brown shorts that came almost to her knees, yet showed her well-exercised, shapely tanned legs. She worked hard to keep herself fit and had succeeded quite well, indeed. Hardly anyone could guess her true age of thirty-three. Above the brown shorts she wore a white cotton, short-sleeved peasant blouse with a small, red and green butterfly embroidered above her right breast. Her medium-length, wavy brown hair hung to her shoulders and she wore dark sunglasses that hid her what he knew to be intelligent, light green eyes.

All in all, she was at the peak of her womanhood—smart, good looking, successful. It was not surprising to him why she was so appealing. He couldn't imagine any man not wanting to be with a woman like her.

"You wanna go on to the Pyramid of the Sun?" he said.

"Sure." She followed him down the walkway and then up and out onto the other side of the *Ciudadela* with its row of pyramid platforms facing a similar row directly across the large open field beyond the temple. They were halfway back to the Avenue of the Dead when she suddenly put her arm out to stop him.

"Wait, listen."

"What?" He looked around the area.

"Can't you hear it?"

He listened intently, for what he didn't know. He heard the cries of vendors, the conversations of tourists, the wind moving through the grass.

"There, hear the wind?"

"Yes," he said.

"It's there. I feel it. I feel them. I see their history, the sacrifices, the priests, the people."

He concentrated all his mental powers on seeing and hearing what she did.

"On the winds of time." She closed her eyes. "They're still alive. Their spirits are still here."

"Yes." He could not feel but imagined the truth of her insight.

In his mind he pictured the *Ciudadela* at its peak, its pyramids brightly painted, its spaces filled with flamboyantly dressed warriors, statesmen, priests, kings.

"What a terrible, beautiful place this has been." She took his hand unbidden.

They stood still for a few moments, eyes closed, listening to the wind, listening to the past. Finally, the sharp cry of a nearby vendor broke the spell. They opened their eyes and looked at each other.

"Thank you for taking me here." She squeezed his hand.

At the Pyramid of the Sun they stopped for several minutes admiring its massiveness and height. He slowly scanned it from its base to the top.

"Too high up for me," she admitted. "Good exercise, but heights bother me."

"Me, too."

"Let's go on to the Pyramid of the Moon."

"Right on." She took his arm once more.

"This is a little more like it," he said when they had reached the symmetrical plaza fronting the Pyramid of the Moon.

"What went on in this area?"

He swept his left arm around to encompass the series of low side by side, facing platform-like pyramids in the plaza. "Supposedly, this was a military and maybe religious parade ground. You can imagine the chiefs and priests of all the local tribes up on these flat-surfaced pyramids with all their warriors in formation at the bases."

"It must have been spectacular," she said.

"And really colorful, too, if the historians are right. It would have really been something to see. As long as you weren't being sacrificed, that is."

"Yeah, as long as."

He stood. "Well, I'm going to go up the Moon. Will you hold my backpack?"

"Sure." She took the day bag from him. "Go ahead. I'll watch you."

She stayed in the center of the plaza and watched him traverse the Pyramid of the Moon. At the first level of the pyramid he stopped, looked for her and finding her, waved. She waved back. From the second level of the pyramid he again waved. She waved back and indicated for him to come down. He signaled okay and after catching his breath began a careful descent.

"Coming down those steps," he said when he had rejoined her on the plaza, "is bad. It looks like you're going straight down and the steps are really tall."

"Let's get something to eat and drink. Besides I want to shop a little for souvenirs before we go."

"All right, sounds good to me. But how about a picture first?"

"Okay." She handed him her camera. "You take me and then I'll take you."

"Good deal."

After the picture taking, they had sodas and sandwiches at a little *tienda* at the head of a series of souvenir shops just outside the archaeological zone. They then spent a good hour or more going from shop to shop, her pricing, selecting, rejecting, sometimes buying, him standing to one side, watching, laughing, admiring, frequently groaning as she purchased this or that mass-produced "artifact."

At the end of the tour, they climbed on board a big bus. They sat together near the front, holding hands and she rested her head on his shoulder. The driver noted them in his rear view mirror. When Stephen caught the man checking them out, he gave him the high sign. The driver winked knowingly.

When they got back to town it was nearly dark and they climbed off the bus slowly, stiffly, quietly happy from their day at the great ruins. They walked past a cathedral near the drop off point and on to the zocalo, the verdant, park-like town square. They had a slow beer together at an outdoor restaurant.

"You're a wonderful guide," she told him.

He slid his chair closer to her; leaned toward her for a kiss, but she turned so that he could only kiss her cheek. As he moved closer still, he felt an odd shaking, a peculiar drifting sensation, followed by what seemed a dark shadow drifting over, blocking, closing out his sight.

—

"Wake up, buddy," a man's voice called to him. He felt the shaking again. Slowly he opened his eyes.

"Lisa?" You're so won...."

"Easy, tiger."

"Tom? What are you doing here?"

"He just got here," Lisa said from just beyond Stephen's vision.

Crap. He must've been saying really stupid stuff coming out of his fever.

"Was I saying really stupid stuff when I came out of my fever?"

"Oh, no." Lisa moved into his line of sight. "You weren't saying anything."

"No?"

"Not since I got here, either," Tom added.

"You look like you're going to be okay now. Now that Tom's here, I think I better go. He can take care of you."

"Thank you, Lisa." Stephen felt a rush of fraternal affection for his friends. For whatever else could be said about him, no one could say he did not have an appreciation for those close to him. And that feeling grew stronger with every experience he shared with them. "I'm sorry you had to go to so much trouble."

"It wasn't any trouble. We're friends. That's what friends do for each other."

"Thank you anyway."

"You're welcome."

"Okay, Tom," Stephen said, almost the second Lisa exited the apartment. "Was I blabbing stupid stuff about Lisa while I was out?"

"Well, you might've called her name a couple of times."

"Oh, jeez."

"And you were mumbling about Mexico or something. What was that about? Did you have dreams?"

"I guess."

Looking down at his wet shirt, he noticed a small wrapper and a small pin, the kind you put on the fronts of ball caps, resting on his clothes. He pulled them out to look at them more closely.

"What do you have there?" Tom said.

Stephen looked at the wrapper. It said El Morro Chocolate. The pin was shaped like the Pyramid of the Sun. Along the bottom of it was the word Teotihuacan. A little chill ran down his back. All he could think of then was getting into the bathroom to take a steaming hot bath or shower. He had to get cleaned up and warm. Get the fever and the dreams out of his system.

"Nothing." He dropped the wrapper and pin under his wet covers. "Nothing at all."

He slowly rose from the couch, wrapping a wet sheet around his wet body and clothes.

"I gotta take a shower or something. I gotta get squared away."

"Sure." Tom helped him stand. "Sure you do, buddy. You've had a rough time of it lately."

"I'd say I have." Stephen nodded in agreement. "I sure as heck have."

HOOVERVILLE

David White, Stephen's father, thought his son's little one bedroom apartment was a cluttered, unkempt mess.

'Your apartment," Mr. White said with mild annoyance, "is a cluttered, unkempt mess."

"What, Dad?" Stephen called from his small kitchen off the main living/dining room area. He was frantically trying to organize the kitchen with its dirty dishes, empty food containers, and refuse that were both a metaphor for and the reality of his distinctly disorganized life. His dad might suddenly decide to look around the place and if he saw the condition of Stephen's kitchen it could lead to a stern lecture on the art of living alone. Stephen wanted to avoid that lecture at all costs.

Out in the living room, his father moved some books around on a messy coffee table. The titles of the books all sounded peculiar to the elder White male.

"Waiting for Lefty?" He picked up a smaller volume. "Ten Days that Shook the World? The Grapes of Wrath. What are you reading," he said loudly, just as Stephen re-emerged from the kitchen, "a bunch of commies?"

"You don't have to yell, dad. I'm right here."

"Yeah. I can see that."

"Why didn't mom come?" Stephen tossed a couple of towels off his undersized couch and sat down.

"Hen stuff."

"Hen stuff?"

"You know, some kind of Lady's Auxiliary crap."

"Oh, I see," Stephen said, not seeing. "Sit down, dad."

"Where?" Mr. White looked askance at the couch.

Stephen jumped up and removed a pair of pants and a shirt from a cheap, padded chair on the other side of the coffee table.

"Great." Mr. White sniffed, but he sat down.

The two men of the White clan of Nevada, Missouri sat across from each other then, silently observing one another over the distance of the book-covered coffee table. When the silence finally became too much for Stephen to bear, he spoke.

"You said something about what I was reading before?"

He knew his father already thought that he was highly suspect when it came to being a man out in the world—a man living, socializing, working, reading on his own.

"I said that this looks like a bunch of commie crap you have piled up here."

"Commie?" Stephen said. "There aren't any commies anymore, Dad. It's just terrorists now. Magic ones, ones that can appear and...."

The look on his dad's face caused Stephen to break off what he thought was a funny little rant. Whoa, Nellie, he told himself, hold up. Don't go there. Don't play the anti-War on Terror card. Not with the old man. He'll go crazy.

"That kind of talk is just plain crazy."

"Sure, pop. I was just trying to make a joke."

"A bad one."

Stephen hushed up. No point in making his dad mad. The old man came by seldom enough as it was.

"You kids nowadays don't have any idea about how things used to be," Mr. White declared. "Why back in my day...."

"I know, you had to walk two miles to school, in a foot of snow, uphill both ways." His father's frown instantly wiped the beginnings of a smile from Stephen's lips.

"You remember your Great-Uncle Mortie Higgins, don't you?"

Stephen remembered Uncle Mortie all right. From the last family reunion where the sawed-off relative had corralled Stephen by a table filled with pies, cakes and cookies baked by the ladies of the White, Higgins, and other families of the clan.

"You young people have no idea what life was like back in the Great Depression." Uncle Mortie had foreshadowed Stephen's dad's comments of moments before.

"You weren't even born yet during the Depression, Uncle Mortie," Stephen foolishly blurted out.

"Not long after, Mr. Know It All," Uncle Mortie countered. "Not so long after. And we lived in the country. We were always in a depression. The big one didn't mean anything to us."

"Uh-huh." Stephen then stupidly made the walking two miles to school remark to Uncle Mortie, too.

"Oh, sure, Mr. Smart Alec," Uncle Mortie said, a little hurt. "Thanks. Mr. Knows Everything."

"I'm sorry, Uncle Mortie."

Luckily for Stephen, just then some music playing members of the family had launched into "Mountain Dew."

"My Uncle Mort, he's sawed off and short...." they sang enthusiastically.

"See there, Uncle Mortie," Stephen said, "they're singing your song."

"Hmmph," Uncle Mortie snorted.

"You should be more respectful of your Uncle Mortie." Mr. White broke into Stephen's reverie.

"I love Uncle Mortie. It's just that he tells tall tales."

"You'll never understand what it was like. You young ones just don't get it."

"You want a coke, dad?" Stephen forcefully drug the two men out of the past and the direction the conversation seemed intent on going.

"I guess. I suppose."

Stephen trundled off into the kitchen to get the cokes. He didn't know why his dad had showed up so early on a Saturday morning but he was definitely not prepared for it.

"How's the job going?" Mr. White called after him.

"Fine, dad." Stephen located a couple of semi-clean tea glasses in a cabinet with an ill-fitting door.

"You got a girlfriend there?"

Stephen took the two glasses out and made a reasonable effort to wipe the stains off their ugly, yellow-flower pattern. Then he located two cans of Coca-Cola Classic.

"Want ice?" He ignored the question about his nearly non-existent social life.

Besides, when the words work and girl were used closely together in a conversation, all Stephen could think about was Lisa Backman, the object of a rather considerable case of his unrequited love.

"I don't want hot soda," his father told him.

"Yes, sir."

Stephen opened the refrigerator and then the little door to the ice compartment. There was some kind of pungent odor in the fridge. He tried to locate the smell but nothing seemed to be too decomposed, nothing had anything green growing on it.

He took a tray of ice out of the compartment and snapped a couple of cubes out into the glasses. The cubes looked a little on the brownish side for clean water but Stephen shrugged it off. He walked back into the living room and handed his father one of the glasses,

"Is this thing clean?" Mr. White suspiciously eyed the ugly tea glass he held in his right hand as if it might be a venomous snake. He turned the glass around several times. "Did you use tap water to make this ice?"

"It'll be all right, Dad," Stephen assured his father, but when he took a big swig of his coke he noticed right away that it tasted funny. A little on the metallic side.

"Your mother and I feel you should get out more often, Stephen." Mr. White took a sip of coke. He scrunched up his nose at the drink and sat it on a nearby counter. "You should be finding a girl soon. Marriage. Grandkids. You know."

"Let's not talk about that, dad." Stephen swallowed a big drink of the funny-tasting soda.

"Well, let me tell you something, mister." His father launched into an all too-familiar routine.

It was all about how he, Stephen, should be saving money, buying a home, going out more often, blah, blah, blah. Mr. White ran this routine by Stephen most every time they got together, which wasn't often, but occurred enough so that Stephen was bored with it.

He sat down on his small couch and leaned back. His dad rattled on. Maybe ten or twelve minutes later, just as Mr. White was really hitting his stride, Stephen began to feel funny—tired, faint, light-headed.

"I don't feel so good," he said so softly that his dad didn't hear him at first. "I think I need to lie down."

"What?" his dad finally paused in the midst of the usual micro-economics lecture he was giving Stephen.

"I'm feeling funny. I think I need to take a nap."

"A nap? Now, this early in the day? What is the matter with you?"

"Gotta rest, dad." Stephen weakly slumped onto the couch. "Need to just take a little nap."

"Well," his father said. "For heaven's sakes."

—

The first thing that penetrated Stephen's senses was the strong, nearby smell of smoke. Wood smoke, he was sure of that. And then the odor of coffee boiling. It smelled really good. Stephen breathed it in deeply, sighed, and opened his eyes.

"Whoa," he cried out, "what the...."

He was at the edge of what looked like, in the gray, pre-dawn light, an old-fashioned hobo jungle. There were maybe ten or twelve men huddled around a fire where the coffee was cooking in an old, black pot on top of wood coals.

"Finally woke up, huh?" a quavery voice to Stephen's right asked.

Stephen, startled yet again, pulled back. The voice belonged to a ragged, dirty old man. There was enough light to see that his shoes and pants were practically worn out. He wore an incongruous, once-expensive coat of a faded plaid color—the shirt beneath it, Stephen assumed, was as worn as his pants and shoes. The old man was missing several front teeth and he had several days, at least, of white-stubble on his chin. Unkempt gray hair poked out from beneath a slick-dirty stocking cap that was either blue or black.

"Wha... are you talking to me?" Stephen choked out.

"Don't know who else it'd be, young feller," the old man said good-naturedly. "You're sitting right here by me, ain't you?"

"Well," Stephen said haltingly, "I guess I am."

"Well, there you are then," the old man said. "Care for some hobo coffee?"

"Hobo coffee?"

"Just old grounds and dirty water in a bottom-burnt pot," the old man explained. "Not bad for what it is."

"Oh, uh, no thank you."

"Polite boy, ain't you? Where you headed, if I may ask?"

Stephen looked around at the other men by the fire. None of them seemed to notice he was there. It was all so strange. He didn't have any idea where he was. Or *when*.

"Where are we?"

"You don't know where we are?"

"No."

"Just outside Tulare."

"Tulare? Where's that?"

"Boy, you don't know much of nothin', do you."

"Uh, no," Stephen admitted.

"California, son." The old man said. "California."

"How'd we get here?"

"On that train over there on the side track."

"Was I with you on the train?"

"You're always with me." The old man said.

"Hey, Buster," one of the other hobos, a big, rough-looking man, called over to the old man. "Talkin' to your imaginary pals again? Hope they kept you warm last night. Maybe they'll help you get a job today."

The rough-looking man and the other hobos laughed heartily. It seemed like it was a long standing joke of some kind.

"You leave me alone," Buster muttered back, then again to Stephen. "Don't pay them no mind, they're just jealous 'cause none of them have friends. They're just bums. Lousy hobos."

"What are you?" Stephen hoped not to sound condescending or rude. Buster didn't take offense.

"Down on my luck," the old man said matter-of-factly. "A lot of us are these days."

Stephen started to form several more questions for the old man, such as when "these days" were, what was going on, and where they were going. But he didn't get the chance to articulate them to Buster because as Stephen was opening his mouth to speak, there was a loud, metallic sound. The sound that trains make when they are beginning to move, when the attached cars are suddenly jerked forward with that first movement. Just as suddenly as the sound came, the hobos around the fire were also in motion.

"C'mon," someone yelled, "she's movin' out. Hurry."

One of the men kicked sandy dirt onto the fire beneath the coffee pot, another grabbed the pot itself, and the whole group raced for the side track where the train was starting to move forward.

"Keep an eye out for Bulls," the rough-looking hobo told the others. "They'll knock our heads and kick us off if they see us."

"Hurry up, Buster," another of the hobos yelled at Stephen's newfound friend.

"I'm comin'," Buster called back, "I'm comin'."

With the old man, Stephen hustled breathlessly towards the creeping train. He'd never ridden the rails and he had no idea how to really hop onto one of the cars. There seemed to be several of the kind with sliding side doors and a couple of open flat cars as well. Buster made a bee line for the last car with an open side door. Stephen was amazed at how easily, and agilely, the old fellow was able to get on board.

While Stephen huffed and puffed alongside the track, Buster reached out a hand. Stephen grabbed it just as the train was starting to pick up speed. With an ungraceful leap only made possible by Buster's help, Stephen launched himself into the railroad car and landed with a side-bruising thud on its dirty, wooden floor.

"My, my," the old man said. "You are a sure-fire rookie at this, yes you are."

—

From the position of the hot sun above, Stephen guessed it was sometime about noon when the train began to slow down again. Fields of crops he couldn't identify rolled by and had been doing so for the last couple of hours as Buster and the handful of hobos in this car dozed or talked quietly among themselves.

Stephen peered out the part-way open railroad car door and tried to determine where the heck they were and where they might be going. Just as he was about to risk showing how dumb he was again and ask Buster where they were, another jolt shook the car and the train began to slow. A couple of the hobos moved up by the door.

"Get ready, boy." Buster slid beside Stephen.

"Ready for what?"

"We gotta jump, son."

"Jump?"

"Stop your jabberin', Buster," one of the other hobos said, as the train slowed up enough for the men to bail out, "you're givin' me the heebie-jeebies." Buster looked at Stephen.

"Jump!" The old man piled out of the train car with the rest of the hobos right behind. Stephen stood at the door, uncertain. "Jump, son, now. Hurry."

Stephen took a deep breath, edged to the doorway, and with eyes closed launched himself out of the car and onto the ground beyond the tracks. To Buster's amusement, Stephen hit hard, rolling across the rocky soil in a dusty whirlwind.

"Whooee," Buster howled, "nice job."

"Crap." Stephen picked himself up, slapping the dirt off his clothes.

"Bulls!" one of the other hobos hollered. "Run for it."

"Bulls?"

"Railroad bulls." Buster explained to Stephen as they hustled after the other hobos. "Railroad police. They'll bust our heads with their clubs if they catch us. Hurry, boy, run."

"I'm running," Stephen exclaimed breathlessly, "I'm running."

Racing through a nearby lettuce field, the rail riders evaded the bulls, and in just a few minutes, Buster and Stephen found themselves temporarily safe in the field, and alone—the other hobos having split off in several directions.

"Where are we going?" Stephen said when they reached a narrow, paved road beyond the big lettuce field. The sun was high in the sky now and it was getting hot.

"I know a place not so far from here. If we can get a ride on this road it's probably not an hour away."

"What kind of place?"

"You'll see."

After about forty-five sweltering minutes walking along the one-lane blacktop road, a big flatbed truck came by with several men riding in back. They slowed up to let Buster onboard and Stephen leapt up alongside his new mentor.

"You'll like this place we're goin' to," Buster said when the truck continued on down the road. "Food, water, good people. It's all right."

"Who you talkin' to, old man?" one of the other men in the bed of the truck said to Buster.

"Don't mind him," another man offered, "that's just old Buster. Everybody knows he's crazy. Don't pay him no mind."

"Hmmph," Buster snorted. "Crazy my eye."

Stephen curled up against the wood sideboards of the truck and tried to get some rest. He didn't have any doubt that there was a crazy person there in the back of that truck—he just wasn't so sure it was old Buster.

—

"Here we are," Stephen heard Buster say maybe an hour after they had begun their hitched truck ride.

"Here we are where?" Stephen opened his eyes to take in his new surroundings. Buster held out both his own arms as if he were presenting some great wonder of the world.

Stephen was amazed to see the number of people along the side of the road as the truck slowed up, moving maybe five miles an hour. And beyond the road on either side, shacks and more people. Shacks made of scrap wood and pieces of metal, held together with bailing wire or reclaimed nails.

Stephen heard laughter and talk and singing. It was a busy, bustling, convivial-seeming place. There were children running around, threadbare clothes hung on makeshift wire lines strung between trees or vehicles, fires over which sat large black pots from which steam rose into the air above the haphazardly thrown together living spaces. He was sure he smelled beans, and maybe bacon, cooking. It made his mouth water, but he realized for the first time that, oddly enough, he was neither hungry nor thirsty.

"What is this place?"

The old man showed a snaggle-toothed smile.

"Hooverville, son. Welcome to Hooverville."

Buster got himself a handout of hot beans, bread, and a cupful of water from an accommodating family, then he and Stephen walked to a clearing beside a small creek that ran on the west side of the Hooverville.

"How come there are so many people here, Buster?" Stephen said after the old man had settled himself on an old bucket turned upside down for a seat.

"There's a famous union man comin' in after a while. Leastways that's what I gathered from some of the talk around the food pots."

"They build this place just for that?"

"No, boy." Buster sighed. "You don't know nothin' hardly a'tall, do ya?"

"I'm sorry."

"Well, heck, son, these here places are all over the country. It's where all the out of work folks gather together to try and survive. Most of the men, and sometimes some of the women, are here to try and find work in these fields for the rich farmers that own them. They're just tryin' to survive. Get enough food to stay alive. Together they figure they can make it. By themselves there ain't no chance."

"This union guy coming in, did they say who he was?"

"He's a famous singer, too, I here tell. He has to move in and out of these places fast 'cause the bosses are after him and maybe the G-Men, too."

"Wow." Stephen whistled, the hint of something familiar about this strange new situation lightly piquing his thoughts. "He must be some kind of guy."

"I reckon we're gonna find out soon enough," Buster pointed out to the road that split the Hooverville in two.

"How do you mean?"

"Because here he comes right now."

In a moment, people gathered all around, laughing, talking, craning their necks for some sight of the singing union man. The entire Hooverville was suddenly ablaze with excitement.

"There he is," someone cried out.

"It's Sonny Jacobs," another voice chimed in.

Then, in a cloud of rolling dust, a rattletrap pickup truck rumbled into the makeshift town. The crowd ran towards the truck as one, Buster and Stephen hurtling forward with them. Buster wove in and out of the crowd, trying to make it to the front. Stephen, ever mindful of being discovered, followed closely but took great pains not to touch anyone. It was a difficult task that suddenly became simple when the crowd parted—as if this Sonny were Moses and the people the Red Sea—and the great man appeared in the midst of the throng.

"Howdy, folks." Sonny addressed the crowd with a wave. He wore his guitar slung over one shoulder like it were a weapon of some sort. "Ready for some old fashioned union building, some comrade to comrade solidarity?" The crowd roared its approval.

"Yee haw," Buster hollered, not five feet from the legendary Sonny, "it's you. It's you for sure."

"It's me, pops." Sonny grinned at the old man's exuberance. "Here I am."

"I'll be dadblamed." The old man reminded Stephen for all the world of the old western sidekicks he'd seen or heard about from the old cowboys movies. Guys with names like Frosty, Smiley, Dusty, Gabby, and ... Buster.

"C'mon, pops," Sonny said to Buster, "help me get ever'body all rounded up over here by the creek. I'll sing 'em a song or two and then get to some union work."

"You betcha, Sonny." Buster happily displayed his gap-toothed smile.

With the old man's help, Sonny soon had the crowd circled around him on the side of the Hooverville nearest the creek that served as both the community's source of drinking water and, less wholesomely, its cleaning area and waste dump. Stephen, no longer even noticed by Buster, stood at the fringes of the crowd and listened raptly to the organizer's mixture of union propaganda and folksy humor and music.

Stephen found the man and his message altogether captivating. Momentarily he was even more captivated by a young woman who was maybe two rows up in the crowd. She had wavy brown hair, a thin body with a surprisingly round bottom, and when she turned around briefly—light, green eyes. Lisa, Stephen thought, she looks like Lisa, or her mom—her grandma?

While he was focused on the young girl, Stephen missed most of what Sonny was saying and singing but a loud surge in the crowd noise brought him back to the man and his message.

"This country," the singer told the crowd, "belongs to us, not them. To each and every one of us. We built it. We worked for it. It's yours and it's mine. From out here in the west all the way to New York City. This land is ours."

The crowd applauded and yelled again and then the sound rose even higher as Sonny swung his guitar around from behind his back and, pulling a pick out of his shirt pocket, started playing and singing one of his songs—an upbeat folksy tune about, naturally enough, workers and unions.

During the latest upsurge in the crowd, Stephen managed to slip up closer to the Lisa look-alike and stood to one side admiring her profile. He froze in place for a moment when, for just a second, she seemed to act as if she knew she were being watched.

Afraid to move and lost in the thrill of the moment, with the elated crowd singing and laughing and swaying back and forth and with the beautiful girl right before him, Stephen did not hear or see the first signs of trouble. They came fast and furious.

Out on the road to the left of the gathering, maybe a half dozen trucks loaded with men armed with sticks and clubs came roaring up. Caught, like Stephen, almost completely off guard, the Hooverville residents had barely begun to realize what was going on before the armed men piled out of the trucks and began to batter anyone in their way—male or female, young or old.

"It's the farmers' goons," a man near Stephen yelled into the general confusion and melee.

While Stephen remained rooted to his spot in the midst of the throng, the girl and everyone else in sight took off running in any direction they could to avoid the truncheon-bearing men who stormed through the mob bashing bodies and heads with a gleeful lack of discrimination.

The union singer man, Sonny, had bolted late and he was harried by the thugs as he raced to catch up and lose himself in the dispersing crowd. As he fled, Sonny's path took him right toward Stephen, who was lock-step riveted to the spot he had been when the ruckus started. He looked up wide-eyed as Sonny came barreling down on him and at the last second before they would have occupied the same position, Sonny shifted his body to avoid a collision. As the two men stared into each other's eyes for the briefest of seconds, Stephen in complete shock, Sonny with a mischievous smile on his face, the singer spoke.

"Here you go, buddy." He flipped something at Stephen as he tore past.

"You can see me?" Stephen called after Sonny, grabbing at the object the singer had thrown. It fell to the ground at Stephen's feet.

"Good luck, kid," Sonny yelled back without looking around.

Amazed at all that was happening, Stephen bent down to pick up the small object by his shoes. He felt in the dirt, felt something kind of hard, but flexible. He started to put the object in his pocket but as he did he looked up just in time to see one of the goons coming right at him with wooden truncheon upraised.

"You're gonna get it, commie," the man shrieked.

Stephen cried out, putting both hands up to block the oncoming blow.

It was too late, the weapon came down straight for the top of his head. And then all was black.

—

Stephen knew he was alive but he was in a dark place. A place that was shaking. Or a place where something or someone was shaking him. An image of people running all around was fresh in his mind, as was the image of some old man. That was it, the old man.

"Stop it, Buster." Stephen fought the darkness to reach the light. "Quit shaking me."

"Buster," a familiar voice sounded in Stephen's returning consciousness, "who the hell is Buster?"

"What?"

"I said, who's Buster?"

"Dad?" Stephen opened his eyes. His head ached and his neck was sore.

"Well, I sure ain't this Buster guy." Mr. White growled down at his son who was supine on the couch in the little apartment that the elder White found so cramped and uncomfortable. "Who are you talking about?"

Stephen took a moment to let his head clear and his eyes focus. The headache and soreness in his neck were quickly dissipating. He thought he might feel all right again in a minute or two.

Stretching backwards he felt something small fall onto the front of his pants. Reaching down slowly for the unseen object, for sure trying to keep his dad from seeing what he was up to, Stephen came up with the object—a guitar pick, old and broken along one edge.

"Sonny Jacobs," he said out loud.

"Good lord," Mr. White said, "now what, or who? Who are you talking about now?"

"No one, dad, forget about it." Stephen pocketed the pick surreptitiously.

His dad didn't need to know about the odd things that happened to Stephen. He already thought Stephen was about the weirdest child a human being could have. No reason to give him any more empirical evidence for that point of view. Not today anyway.

"I tell you," Mr. White said. "I don't understand you sometimes."

"How long was I out?"

"I don't know, maybe five, ten minutes. I wasn't keeping track."

"But you stayed."

"Yeah, I stayed. And now I'm going."

"Not yet, pop, please."

"I gotta get back. What happened to you, anyway?"

"I don't know, dad. I have these little spells from time to time."

"No wonder." Mr. White pointed at the books he'd criticized before on the messy coffee table by the couch. "This commie crap will ruin your mind."

Stephen started to work up a counter argument in his head but thought better of it. There was no point in getting into useless fights with his dad. The old man had his ways and he had his. It was up to one of them to find a way past their differences without tearing each other up in the process.

"Can you hang with me for just a few more minutes?" Stephen said quietly. His dad gave him a funny look and shuffled around uncomfortably.

"You're an awfully strange boy, Stephen, did you know that?"

"Yeah, I know that, pop, but I'm trying to be better."

Stephen thought about how the folks at the camp had treated one another.

He'd learned from them the value of togetherness, of helping one another out, of caring for each other.

"Well."

"I'd appreciate it."

"There's probably nothing going on at home but hen stuff anyway. What the hay."

"Thanks, dad," Stephen said. "That's great. Thanks."

"Yeah, sure." Mr. White looked around the apartment as if he didn't know where the doors were through which he could escape if need be. "You bet. Okay."

DOOR GUNNER

"Nothing like getting out on a day like today is there, Stephen?"

Stephen White and his Uncle Carl walked across the stubble of a long-since harvested cornfield about seven miles from their hometown of Nevada, Missouri. It was a beautiful mid-fall day, sunny, just warm enough to be comfortable, with a deep blue sky above that was only occasionally streaked with long wisps of high cirrus clouds. The two men had been out for maybe forty-five minutes, carrying shotguns loaded with bird shot in an ostensible search for quail. Mostly they were just walking and talking.

"It's really beautiful." Stephen paused to take in the world around them.

Carl was Stephen's father's older brother and he had made it an infrequent task of his to get his slightly pudgy nephew out of the younger man's claustrophobic apartment and out into the real world—preferably doing something that would improve the boy's dubious outdoors skills.

Carl took him fishing at least once in the summer and tried but usually failed to get him to go deer hunting in the winter. Sometimes in the early spring he convinced the boy to go on a day canoeing trip or a hike along the banks of the Marais des Cygnes River north of Nevada. In the fall he had some success convincing Stephen to go bird hunting, mostly because they both liked to walk the country fields in the cooler weather—even if they didn't get any birds, which they seldom did.

For today's putative hunt, Carl carried his own nearly new .410 gauge Remington 870 pump-action shotgun. The 870s, in whatever gauge, were the perfect inexpensive shotgun for the average hunter or casual blue rock shooter. Carl had brought a different .410 for Stephen. It was an old side-by-side, double-barrel .410, from some company down in South America. It was a fun little shotgun, if used properly.

Its only drawback was that it had a sensitive left barrel trigger that had, in addition to a near hair trigger action, the added "feature" that sometimes when you pulled the quick left trigger both barrels fired at once. It could be disconcerting if you weren't ready for firing even one of the barrels.

"I ought to apprise you, Stephen, that your little .410 there has a sensitive left trigger. You might want to be careful with it."

"You mean …." Stephen immediately discharged both barrels of his little bird gun into an upraised dirt heap in one of the rows of the field not six feet out in front of himself and Carl.

"Holy cow!" Carl reeled backwards across a row directly behind the two men. "What are you trying to do, pull a Dick Cheney on me?"

"I… I… I'm sorry, Uncle Carl."

Carl White was a combat veteran of the Vietnam War and Stephen knew his uncle well enough to understand that the ex-soldier's reactions to things, particularly a gun going off right next to him, might trigger a strong response.

Carl made no bones about suffering from Post Traumatic Stress Disorder and had told Stephen once that he got a check every month from the government because he had been rated as being thirty percent disabled as a result of the PTSD.

Stephen's father, David, who had never even been in the service, thought his older brother was just being overly sensitive, even a whiner. Mr. White used to tell Stephen that he thought Carl was at least twenty percent crazy before he even went to that overblown war in Indochina. Stephen knew his uncle well enough to know that Carl didn't really care what anybody, including his own brother David, thought of him.

"It's okay." Carl surprised his nephew by the speed at which he regained his composure after the shotgun blast and by the gentleness of his tone. "You just gotta be more careful with that weapon. But I should've warned you earlier."

"Thanks, Uncle Carl," Stephen said gratefully, "I'm real sorry."

"I tell you what." Carl pulled a small flask of whiskey out of his back pocket, which Stephen knew he always carried with him, and took a short pull on it. "Why don't we head over to the creek and have a snack. If we scare up any quail, fine, if not we'll just grab a bite to eat and have something to drink. Want a hit?"

"I don't think I would've made a good soldier, Uncle Carl." Stephen declined the proffered flask as they headed towards a creek that ran beyond the cornfields. Carl gave his nephew a once over.

"Not everybody is. Heck, Stephen, for each combat troop in the field there used to be ten support personnel. Don't know what it is nowadays, over in the Middle East, probably higher I suspect. And that don't count the Navy and the Air Force people."

"I'm a lousy hunter, too. I feel like a fish out of water." Stephen grinned. "Even at fishing. I don't know why you put up with me."

"I put up with you because you're my nephew, my brother's son. I've known you your entire life. You're an okay guy, Stephen. Not everyone is good at outdoor stuff."

"Yeah, but I really suck."

"You hike around and things like that, don't you?"

"Yeah, some."

"Well."

"Well, thanks anyway."

"For what?"

"For not getting all freaked out by my shooting right in front of us. Dad would've killed me."

"Ah." Carl said. "I've been in a lot worse situations than that. A lot closer calls."

"Yeah?" Stephen wondered as they reached a stand of trees, mostly elm and oak, near the creek beyond the cornfields.

"You bet your fanny. Hell, one time up in Phu Bai some son of a gun opened up a .50 caliber right by my darned ear. I still got tinnitus from it to this day."

"No kidding, your own guy shot right by your ear."

"Sure did."

"That's worse than what I did, maybe?"

"You gotta be careful with weapons, Stephen," Carl said soberly.

"I'm sorry." Stephen was humbled again in recalling his recent, foolish act. "I feel awful about doin' that, Uncle Carl. I could've shot you."

"It's all right. It was an accident. It could've been bad but it wasn't. No one was hurt. Shake it off. Let it go."

"Thanks, Uncle Carl."

"Forget it."

For a couple of minutes the men let their talk drop as they looked for a good place to get down to the creek and have their lunch.

"Here," Carl said, "cut through these bushes, we're just above the creek now."

"Sure." Stephen was glad his uncle seemed to have let the accident just drop.

"There you go." Carl pointed to a big, flat, white rock near the shore of the creek. "Perfect for having lunch on."

"Yeah," Stephen concurred, "great."

Sitting on the big rock, listening to the gurgling sound of the creek, Stephen and Carl had a pleasant lunch of sandwiches—ham and cheese for Carl, bologna and cheese for Stephen—and a sweet dessert of trail mix. Carl downed his food down with a couple of shots of whiskey; Stephen drank water from the hard plastic bottle he carried with him when hiking or caving.

"Do you mind?" Carl said when they had finished their food and settled back for a brief rest before heading back across the cornfields. He produced a plastic baggie and some rolling papers.

"Uh, no."

Stephen knew Carl smoked but it always surprised him when his uncle would just cavalierly display a bag of weed as if it were the most ordinary thing to do in the world. Having come of age in the 1960s, apparently smoking weed was as normal to Carl as having a beer was to men of earlier ages.

"You sure?" Carl expertly rolled himself a thick joint.

"No problem."

Stephen was mildly asthmatic and never smoked, but as long as he was outdoors and not downwind, it was okay with him if others did.

"May 23, 1971," Uncle Carl said after a few puffs.

"What's that?"

The wind had shifted and the smoke from Carl's joint engulfed Stephen. He could smell it and feel it working its way up into his nasal passages. He sniffed and lightly blew air out his nose.

"That's the last firefight I was in," Carl explained. "We were pinned down just after getting dropped into a hot LZ—landing zone to you. Charlie was everywhere. We lost seven men in ten minutes. Three killed, four wounded. I got out of the clearing and ran behind a tree. Charlie knew I was there. I could hear the rounds hitting off the backside of that tree."

Stephen coughed. He was suddenly struggling to breathe and was getting lightheaded. He tried to shift around but the smoke seemed to follow him no matter what he did. It really started to get to him.

"They really opened up on us after that ..." Carl went on.

"I'm not feeling so good," Stephen interrupted.

"You okay?"

"I don't feel ... my nose..."

"Here, lean back, rest a second. I'll put this out."

Carl stubbed out the joint on the rock and helped his nephew lay back. Stephen could still smell the pungent odor of the weed as it coursed its way up through his nose and into his sinuses. Things started to spin slightly then, causing him to feel dizzy and a little sick to his stomach.

"I'll just rest here, I'll just lie...."

Carl leaned forward to hear what his nephew was saying but there was only the sound of the younger man's breathing. He was out cold.

—

When Stephen opened his eyes, slowly, taking several moments to make sure the world had stopped spinning and that he no longer felt dizzy or nauseated, he found that he was lying on a cot in what looked like a small military barracks. There were a few rows of neatly made up and ordered cots facing each other in front and to the right of where he sat.

On the wall directly before him hung a couple of banners proclaiming unit names and missions—at least that was Stephen's guess as to what they were. There were a lot of numbers and names linked together, anyway.

Careful not to move too quickly, he eased up into a sitting position on the cot. At the moment there seemed to be only one guy in the barracks; he sat on a bunk in front and to the right of the one on which Stephen now sat. The barracks building, Stephen noticed, looked like it was one-half of a large tin can cut vertically and then laid on its side. A Quonset hut, that's what this was, a Quonset hut barracks.

The guy on the other bunk, wearing a light green camouflage uniform, was reading a *Playboy*. Stephen squinted to see but couldn't read the date on the magazine. The cover had a sort of old-fashioned look to it and Stephen figured it was an old one, though why he thought that was not so clear. The other guy was definitely military, Stephen told himself, noticing stripes on the arms of the soldier's fatigue shirt and a patch with an eagle or something on it up closer to the shoulder.

Just as Stephen was getting his bearings in his new environment, feeling a little relaxed perhaps, hoping nothing unsettling was going to happen, the door of the barracks was pushed open roughly and another young man came bursting in. This fellow seemed to be the polar opposite of the quiet young man sitting on his cot reading the *Playboy*. The new arrival was jumpy, jittery, and ready to explode verbally.

"Can you believe this bull, Travis?" The new guy practically hopped up onto the other soldier's cot.

At least he was speaking English. Stephen recalled some of his other odd interludes of recent times. That was a good thing.

"Take it easy, Cantrell," Travis said.

"We gotta go out again today," Cantrell exclaimed as if the order were a crime not just against him and Travis but against the humanity itself. "That's four straight days. That ain't right. What about Jones and Watson. When they gotta do the door? Huh, tell me that, Billy. When?"

"Jones and Watson are door for somebody else."

"I don't see why it's us, again." Cantrell flapped his hands around without hearing what Travis said.

"Damn it, Dave." Travis lowered his magazine. "You do this every time when you know we're going up. Why? Couldn't you try something a little different for a change?" Cantrell reached over and bent the *Playboy* towards himself.

"Look at those boobs." He grabbed his crotch. "Oh, man, I'd crawl on my hands and knees over forty miles of broken glass to hear her fart over a pay phone."

"Funny." Travis pulled the magazine away. "Never heard that before."

"They're nuts." Cantrell abruptly resumed what Stephen assumed was some kind of ritual complaint. Mostly Stephen was just glad neither man seemed to notice he was there. This might be interesting if no one would pay him any mind. "They're messin' with us," Cantrell ranted on. "They're trying to hurt us, Billy. They are seriously interfering with our safety."

"Relax." Travis tried to hide behind the *Playboy*.

"I'm not kidding. I had a dream last night."

"Terrific. I don't suppose I'm going to hear about it." Travis turned the Playboy sideways to get a better look at a picture.

"It was Reynolds," Cantrell pushed on, "Lt. Reynolds. He was jockeying a Cobra, not a regular Huey, you know what I mean?" Travis grunted. "I don't know why, man, but dig, you know what he had for a face? You know what he looked like?

"You doin' speed again, Cantrell?" Travis pitched the *Playboy* aside. "You know how that messes you up. Why don't you ever just smoke a joint and calm down a little?"

"Never mind that," Cantrell rattled on, "it was Reynolds, you know. And he was sort of in a mist and his face was like . . . like a skull and bones. Like on a pirate flag, you dig?"

"You talk trash, Dave." Travis grimaced. "You gotta knock it off. It's bad karma, man. You been droppin' acid or mesc, ain't you? You are such a screw-up."

"I don't want to go with Reynolds and Blaid today, Billy."

"Shut up, Dave."

"I don't wanna go."

"Who in the hell does?"

"I only got 187 days left. I gotta be aware of shit."

"And how many do I have, Dave?" Travis said. Cantrell shrugged. "Seventy-three, bird brain. So stop coming in here every day with your freaked out, doped up BS. You're goin' to jinx us. Now cool it."

Cantrell shut up, but Stephen watched as the uptight door gunner milled around the Quonset hut like a worm in a bait box. He riffled through Travis' magazines and cheesecake clippings, sat down on another cot for a minute but kept tapping his foot on the floor until Travis threatened to throttle him if he didn't stop. He got up again then and paced back and forth. Finally, the exasperated Travis apparently had all he could stand.

"C'mon, Cantrell." He picked up his gear. "Let's get ready to go."

"All right, let's go, let's get out of here. Let's get some chow and then go kick some Charlie butt." Travis led the way out of the barracks.

Stephen hurried after them. This was a new kind of experience for him and he observed the soldiers and their world with considerable interest. He felt mostly comfortable for a change. He was like a fly on the wall with Travis and Cantrell. They didn't seem to be aware of his presence at all. I like this, Stephen told himself. This isn't bad at all. Ahead of him, the two young men finished their apparently daily pre-flight conversational routine.

"You're crazier than a damn loon, you know that, don't you, Cantrell?"

"Sure." Cantrell slapped the sides of his legs repeatedly. "Sure, sure, you bet."

—

Lt. Reynolds, Stephen learned by listening to Travis and Cantrell as they climbed onto the craft, was the pilot of a troop-filled Huey helicopter that would soon be soaring above the lush green Vietnamese countryside. Reynolds and his co-pilot, Chief Warrant Officer Two, Artie "Razor" Blaid, were hauling seven soldiers packed into the chopper like camouflaged sardines to what the crew had been assured was a cool, if not cold, LZ.

When the chopper lifted off, Stephen felt his stomach drop as if he were on a ride at Three Flags or the county fair. He let out a little whoop into the thumping, roaring sound of the elevating helicopter but immediately cut off his cry when Cantrell turned in his direction. The edgy soldier cocked his head to one side as if he might have seen something and Stephen froze. When Cantrell finally looked away, Stephen let out a deep breath and settled back down in the corner of the helicopter where he'd found a helmet with what looked like an intercom hookup to it. Carefully, Stephen slipped the helmet on. No one seemed to notice.

Up front and to the right was Travis, the crew chief. He manned a side door machine gun, an M-60 Stephen heard it called. Cantrell, keyed up like a marionette on Dexedrine, was at the gun on the other side of the ship. Even though nothing was happening, he swung the M-60 back and forth, mumbling and acting like he was firing it. A couple of the riflemen watched him with raised eyebrows.

Behind the ship, Stephen could see from the position he had taken facing backward toward the open doors of the helicopter, came five more Hueys in something resembling a formation.

"It's a beautiful country, ain't it, Artie," Stephen heard Lt. Reynolds say through the intercom, "look out across there. Those hills are beautiful, and see how the river winds along. You'd never know there was a war going on from up here, huh?"

"Yeah, real beautiful. And in about two seconds' time it'll just get itself altogether and blow your ass to kingdom come, that's all. Those green hills are full of Charlie and every sampan you see on the river's probably full of sappers heading for the nearest fire base. It's a regular paradise, a Garden of Eden."

"Oh, Razor, man," Reynolds said. "What a bad attitude you have. It would behoove you to lighten up, troop."

"Horse hockey," Blaid retorted, "smell the napalm, you mean. Smell the burnt out ground, smell the water buffalo shit."

Stephen was amazed at the sardonic attitude the men took in the face of potential deadly combat. It was amazing.

"Say, Cap'n," Stephen heard Travis say into his helmet mike minutes later, adopting a familiar tone and using the nickname the lieutenant apparently allowed him, "how much longer to the LZ? We gettin' there?"

"What's up?" Reynold's asked. "you got a hot date back in Bin Tranh?"

"No, sir. Cantrell's back here doing his silent war movie thing again. Some of our OD natives are getting a little restless." Cantrell's voice came on, sharp and whining.

"Squealer," he complained, "turncoat."

"You boys cool it back there." Reynolds chuckled. "We'll have to leave you out there at the LZ."

"No way, sir," Cantrell said, "this baby bird is my home, this '60 is my broom to clean up the VC cockroaches."

"Just keep a sharp eye, troops," Reynolds said, "we got about another fifteen minutes. Cantrell, why don't you do something like listen to Radio Hanoi, maybe it'll get you keyed up for the LZ. Travis, you tell those restless ground pounders back there to look out the other door if they don't find Mr. Cantrell appealing. Where they're going, he'll be the last normal thing they see for days."

"Yes, sir, Cap'n."

Stephen watched Travis turn and tap the shoulders of the two GIs who had been so interested in Cantrell. They looked around at the crew chief.

"Over there, boys," he yelled into the roar of the chopper, pointing out his door, "look at that." The two GIs leaned over to look out. Stephen craned his neck to see as well.

"See that river? That way, south, the river runs all the way past Saigon. No combat, no sappers, no incoming—bars, women, booze—paradise. Ain't it a beautiful sight?"

The GIs shook their heads. Travis gave them the thumbs up sign. Stephen was filled with admiration and even affection for these brave young men. They were definitely cool.

Over on the other side of the chopper, Cantrell kept jumping around, swinging the M-60 from side to side. He was cursing Reynolds and Blaid as loudly as he could. His words were lost in the rushing wind and the whump-whump-whumping of the chopper rotary blades.

—

The Huey was about two-thirds of the way into the descent, as Stephen understood from Lt. Reynold's dialogue with the crew, when the radio squawked the excited warnings of a radio man somewhere in the tall grass below the chopper. For the first time, Stephen felt the excitement, the adrenalin rush of the situation.

"Blackhawk 1-6-5, this is Charlie Sierra Tango, we got fire down here," the voice crackled in the intercom, "you got a hot LZ. Charlie's firing from everywhere. We're releasing smoke now."

"Blackhawk 1-6-5 to Charlie Sierra Tango," Lt. Reynolds called back, "I see yellow smoke west of the river. Confirm."

"Blackhawk," the radio man responded, "this is Charlie Sierra Tango. Affirmative, sir, on the yellow smoke."

"We're comin' in, Charlie Sierra," Lt. Reynolds said, "give us a fix on Charlie."

"He's all over the place, Blackhawk," the excited voice answered.

"Take it easy, Charlie Sierra," Lt. Reynolds said calmly, "tell us where they're at, soldier. We got five birds here. That's ten '60s laying down support fire."

"Yes, sir," the radio man said, "they're out in front of us, sir, about a click and a half to the south and east towards the river, and a click to the north along the tree line."

"Atta boy, Charlie Sierra," Lt. Reynolds told the radio man, "we're comin' in, now." Then to his crew: "Cantrell, Travis, lay it down straight across to the river and up to the left at the trees, I'll swing around as we descend."

"Yes, sir," Travis called back, breathless.

Suddenly, as the chopper dropped below the trees, the air was filled with metallic whishes. Stephen curled up in a cocoon of his own arms and legs. This was getting to be a little too real now. It was not so much fun. He no longer felt like a fly on the wall. Those were real bullets flying all around. Throughout the rest of the chopper, the reaction of the soldiers was a general, loud cursing.

"Damn it," Razor Blaid spit into his mike, "Travis, Cantrell, get your butts on those 60s. Fry the bastards, get'em off our tail."

As the chopper wobbled and whipped around under Lt. Reynolds' control, Travis and Cantrell strafed the target areas. Sweat poured from their faces and the M-60 barrels smoked from overwork. Reynolds brought the Huey down with a solid thump and the grunts began leaping out into the grass, screaming and firing. Stephen stayed where he was, curled up like a ball. There was no way he could have gone out that door himself. These guys were unbelievable.

Within seconds, the enemy zeroed in on the LZ. A row of holes exploded across the side of the chopper nearest Travis. On Cantrell's side, closer to Stephen's position, a tracer round hammered into an empty metal ammo box. The round stuck there, its blazing phosphorus eating into the box. Cantrell kicked at it, managed to get some of it out the door, but was too busy firing to worry it further. Then another row of holes appeared on the side of the chopper, this time right by Cantrell's door.

Stephen dared a quick look and saw the paint and metal fly from the side of the chopper, heard the whizzing of other rounds near his own head. Then there was a powerful lurch, nearly knocking the door gunners down and the chopper lifted off.

"Atta way, Reynolds," Cantrell cried out, "get this baby out of here."

Of a sudden, Cantrell spun around and saw a GI huddled on the floor, unwilling or unable to budge.

"Damn you," Cantrell screamed, letting go of his M-60, which bounced crazily up and down on the cable securing it above the door of the chopper. "Get out."

He grabbed the soldier and kicked him towards the door. The chopper had risen better than six feet off the ground by the time Cantrell's prodding got the reluctant troop out the door. The soldier crashed into the tall grass below and disappeared. Stephen felt profoundly sorry for the young grunt.

Cantrell, the incident already apparently forgotten, grabbed his M-60 and began firing again. He cursed and howled as he fired. Empty casings flew all over the craft. Some of them landed by Stephen.

In his wild firing, Cantrell didn't seem to hear or notice as another burst of enemy fire banged against the side of the Huey behind him. He just kept shooting out into the Vietnamese countryside below. Stephen thought this young man must be the maddest human he had ever seen.

At last free of its load, the chopper rose, spinning, twisting away from the LZ, toward the protective sky. Reynolds pushed the Huey as hard as he dared. They swung out, climbed, climbed, out of reach of ground fire, flew away, back towards the relative safety of the base camp. Cantrell kept spraying bursts at the receding forest until he heard Reynolds calling over the intercom.

"Travis, Cantrell, everybody cool, everything okay?"

"Oh, my God," Cantrell pushed the M-60 away and held both hands on his helmet, "we're alive. L-T, we're alive."

"That was a little fierce, eh, boys?" Reynolds said into the mic. "Yep. A little intense."

"Hot damn," Cantrell celebrated, "we kicked some VC butt, dudes. Hey, Billy. Hey, man, whad'ya say?"

"Hey, Travis," Blaid came on, "what's up back there?" There was no reply.

"Cantrell," Reynolds' worried voice sounded in the intercom, "what's up back there? Check on Travis." Cantrell was already at Travis' side.

"Billy," he said, "Billy, what the—"

Stephen dared rise. He took off the intercom helmet, crawled carefully forward to a position just to Cantrell's right, off his shoulder. Below them, Travis lay on his back, one leg bent at the knee, the other sticking out the door beneath his free hanging M-60. The barrel of the weapon—now still and checked by its cable restraint—pointed uselessly out at the bright sky.

Travis' jump suit was torn in a half-moon running from his upper left thigh into his groin and across his lower abdomen; the cloth mingled with pumping blood. Cantrell gulped down a small cry. He held Travis against his side, blood staining his flight suit. The chopper rotaries thump-thump-thumped into the humid Vietnamese air.

Stephen leaned over, foolishly reached down towards the fallen door gunner. Cantrell released Travis' body and turned towards Stephen.

"You can see me?" Stephen said to the grieving soldier. "Now?"

"God almighty," Cantrell yelled, jumping up. Stephen began to back away.

Cantrell looked around for something to defend himself with, found a heavy crescent wrench wedged into a cubby hole, lunged at Stephen. Stephen hurried backwards, clumsily. Cantrell stormed at him wildly, wrench raised like a war axe.

"Don't," Stephen cried out, "don't hit me."

Cantrell shrieked unintelligibly, swinging the wrench right at Stephen's head.

Stephen held his arms up defensively. The last thing he saw was the wrench coming right at his face. He turned away at the last second.

—

As Stephen climbed up through the layers of darkness towards consciousness, he became aware of someone calling his name and that he was being lightly tapped on the cheeks. Finally he opened his eyes. It was his Uncle Carl.

"Stephen. Are you okay?"

"I'll be all right. Let me get my breath."

"Sure."

After a few moments he began to feel better, to collect himself, to shake the cobwebs from his mind. He realized he was lying flat on the big white rock by the creek, right where he'd been when they had lunch. He reached an arm up to Carl who helped him to a sitting position.

"You gonna be all right?"

"Yeah." Stephen took several long, deep breaths. "I'm feeling better now."

"Don't rush it," Carl advised.

"No."

After a few more minutes Stephen thought he might feel well enough to try and stand. Again Carl helped him up.

"What happened to you? One minute we were talking and the next you were out."

"How long was I gone?"

"Just a couple of minutes."

"Really?"

"Where did you go? That was a rather strange thing."

Stephen formed an explanation in his mind but stopped before speaking it. In the past few months since he'd started having these "episodes," no one had really directly questioned him about them.

Carl and the others, his mom and dad, his friends Tom Harris and Lisa Backman from work, most everyone, considered him something of an oddball, a weirdo. What would they think of him if he told them the places he'd seen and been since he started having these incidents? They'd think he was a complete nut, worse even than they already did.

"Nowhere," he heard himself tell perhaps the only person who might understand what he had been experiencing. "I didn't go anywhere. I just kind of fainted, blacked out, you know?"

"Hmm." Carl made a doubtful noise.

Stephen felt kind of bad not being honest with Uncle Carl about what really happened. Maybe he would another time. But not today. Not just yet.

He knew he'd learned one thing from this experience—to be more understanding of men like Uncle Carl, men who'd faced death in combat, men who suffered from that experience the rest of their lives. He made a promise to himself to at least be more appreciative, more grateful to the men who had fought for the nation.

"You ready to go back?"

"If you feel up to it," Carl said, "we could go on."

"Let's go."

"Lead on, MacDuff."

Stephen began collecting the things he'd brought along for the day. He picked up the little prematurely-fired .410 and turned to go. As he did, he saw some dark coppery object down by where he'd lain. Bending to it, he had a slight surge of panic. It was a casing from a large shell round. Something the size of, he imagined, a big army machine gun, the kind used by Huey helicopter door gunners in Vietnam.

Turning to block his movements from Carl, Stephen popped open his little .410 and slipped the two spent shells out, letting them drop onto the rock at his feet. As he reached down to pick up the two shotgun shell casings, he nimbly snagged the machine gun casing as well and, giving it a quick once-over, put the shell in his pants pocket.

"What you doing there?" Carl wondered.

"Just making sure I'm unloaded for the walk back."

"Good. Shall we head on home then?"

"Sure." Stephen felt the large caliber casing against his leg. "Let's get out of here. Let's go home."

THE LAST ONE

"I'm not sure it was such a good idea to come to the zoo," Stephen told Tom and Lisa after they had driven up from Nevada to the Kansas City Zoo in Swope Park.

"Nonsense," Lisa said. "You need to get out more often and this is a nice little zoo."

"I hear the one in Omaha is a lot nicer."

"Three more hours of driving," Tom said.

"The neighborhood around here looked tough."

"Stop it," Lisa chided Stephen. "Just because you see a couple of hip-hop looking guys does not mean you're going to get jumped or something."

"We're in the zoo now, anyway."

"I guess so."

"C'mon," Lisa said enthusiastically, "let's go see the African exhibits. I want to see the rhino and the elephants."

"Things are far apart," Stephen complained. "It's a really long walk to some of this stuff."

"Good heavens." Lisa rolled her eyes in dismay. "You want some cheese with that whine?"

Tom fake rough-housed Stephen to try and get the big guy out of his funky mood. "If you look around, you can see that they are working on the walking problem as we speak." He pointed to where the construction of a train system between exhibits was in full swing.

"Actually, Stephen," Lisa commented as the three friends made their way through the zoo grounds, "all this walking is actually good for you. You've lost some weight lately, don't think I didn't notice, and this will help you keep it off and firm it up."

Without realizing it, Stephen tucked in his tummy and pushed his chest out at Lisa's complimentary words. He held his head high and proud.

"Lookin' good, buddy." Tom punched him in the shoulder.

"Cut it out." Stephen acted shy, but he was thrilled by the notice he was getting, especially from the lovely Lisa.

She noticed I dropped some pounds, he applauded himself inwardly. Cool. Most excellent. He remembered the first time he ever saw Lisa Backman, on her first day at Animatec. She wore a stylish, dark suit jacket that matched her professional length skirt and from that moment Stephen thought she was about the prettiest, and sexiest, woman he'd ever known.

It was an unspoken given between the three work friends that Stephen adored Lisa. It was totally one-sided and unrequited on Stephen's part, but Lisa treated him extremely well, like a hip older sister or really good friend. Although he would always want more from their relationship, he was happy any time he was in her company—any time.

"Hey." Tom's voice broke into Stephen's thoughts. "Let's stop here and grab a bite to eat before we go on."

Stephen refocused on the here and now and saw that they had reached a small concession area. Hamburgers, hot dogs, corn dogs, snow cones. That sort of thing.

"Good idea," Lisa said. "I could go for some chow. How about you, Stephen?"

"Uh, yeah. Sure."

"Don't get too excited." Tom said.

"No," Stephen replied. "I can eat a little. Get something to drink."

"Excellent," Lisa said.

Not five minutes after they ate—Tom got a burger and fries, Lisa a chicken sandwich—Stephen felt his stomach begin growling and rumbling. He looked around for restrooms. Luckily there was a facility nearby.

"Where you goin'?" Lisa said when Stephen hustled away.

He covered his mouth to control a sudden onslaught of belching, the foul smell of the greasy corndog he had consumed emanating from him like a noxious gas.

"Be right back." He burped over his shoulder.

"What's up?" Tom asked Lisa.

"Don't know. I think he's just going to the restroom."

Stephen's good fortune held with him in the restroom and although there were a couple of other guys inside, he found an empty stall. As he sat down, he released a really loud belch. So loud that the other patrons hurried about their business and got out of the building.

"Ohh," Stephen groaned, "I feel crappy."

With a big, gaseous sigh, he leaned back as far as he could on the stool and closed his eyes. His body swayed slowly from side to side. He began to feel worse, belching not so loud, but more often, and then he started to feel light-headed. He took one last deep breath, slumped backwards on the stool, and went out.

—

Stephen opened his eyes to the glare and heat of a blazing sun directly overhead. He was sweating profusely and his head hurt. There was an uncomfortable scratchiness in the back of his throat and a nasty, metallic taste in his dry mouth.

"I feel like hell," he said out loud to no one but himself.

Looking around, he saw that he was seated in a Land Rover-type vehicle stopped at the top of a hill, barren except for browning grass and weeds. Beyond him, the countryside looked like it had been in a prolonged drought. The great orange-red ball of the sun had so parched and dried the soil it seemed the earth itself had withered to the point of death. There were no people, nor animals, in sight. He was by himself.

Checking inside the vehicle, he found a clipboard with what looked like official documents on it. "Poachers Reported," the top paper had written on it—in his own hand—"Northeast Quadrant. Investigate. Verify or Dismiss."

Poachers? Where *was* he? Then he checked the papers again. Kintara Game Preserve, Kenya.

"Kenya," he again said out loud, "my God."

With sweat beading up on his forehead, Stephen bent to wipe it off with the sleeve of his shirt. In doing so, he realized he was wearing a uniform. A khaki-colored outfit of jungle shorts, with several big pockets, and matching short-sleeved shirt. Next to him in the front seat was a large bush hat. His size. It occurred to him, then, to look at himself in the rearview mirror.

"I'm a game warden, for cryin' out loud," he said to the mirror. "And," after tilting the mirror to get a fuller view of himself, "I'm tall and muscular. Cool."

He picked up the clipboard, and between glances at his new self in the mirror, flipped through the rest of the pages of what was obviously a log of recent activities. He had been driving around the preserve for days, his notes told him, in search of the poachers who had come to Kintara during this terrible dry season in their new, shining Land Rover, searching for the last one and staying just one step ahead of him.

"The last one?" he wondered. That wasn't altogether clear from the notes.

There was another smaller notebook on the dash and he took that down to look through as well. It only had a few items in it but he found that he had come to resemble the land over which he watched, sick and burning. It seemed that he had picked up a fever during a visit to a local tribe and it was clinging to him like the plague. It made him feel unlucky and weak, he had written, and he assumed his condition was a delight to the poachers. Next to the word poachers was written—The Kudu Bar, evening.

That was certainly a mystery but he felt a strange imperative to seek this place out, find the poachers and confront them. And get something to drink. He was burning up and his throat was dry. Licking his lips, he looked around the vehicle for water but there was only a tiny warm swig at the bottom of a small bottle. Without understanding how or why he was doing the things he was doing, he started up the vehicle and just took off driving—letting his destination be a matter of instinct rather than thought.

—

It was sometime after nine, according to the clock on the wall behind the counter, when he walked through the door of the Kudu. With his first glance around the bar, he spotted the poachers. It was obvious who they were and that they had been waiting for him. They were drinking rum and laughing loudly, arrogantly. Apparently they felt no need to hide who they were or what they were after.

When he walked in, the laughing dwindled and they watched him with a mixture of caution and hostile arrogance. He knew from the clipboard notes he'd seen in his vehicle that he was the head game warden and even though he was sick, in this body he felt strong enough to take the poachers on.

"Evenin'," the bartender said as Stephen stepped up and rested a boot atop the brass railing that ran the length of the wooden bar. "Looks like you got company." He made a short nod of the head in the direction of the poachers. Stephen gave the men a brief, casual look.

"How long they been here, Eddie?" he turned away from the glare of the poachers. It occurred to him that he had no idea how he knew the bartender's name, but he did.

"I dunno, maybe an hour, hour and a half. They're real cuties. Quite a trio."

"The usual?" Eddie picked up a glass and began to shine it with a clean dish rag.

"Huh? Uh, yeah—I mean, no. No, give me something cool. I need something cool right now. How about a gin with tonic water? Lots of ice."

"Coming right up."

Eddie went down to the end of the bar and made the drink. Stephen surveyed the poachers again. They talked loudly when they saw him look over and when he turned back to the bar, one of them, wearing an Aussie bush hat tilted low over his eyes, rose and headed toward him.

"Here you go, my friend." Eddie handed Stephen the gin and tonic. "Nice and cool and on the house."

The poacher with the Aussie hat pulled up to Stephen's right a few feet down the bar. Stephen took a long pull on the drink and sighed deeply.

"Thanks, Eddie, tastes great."

"And cool," Eddie offered.

"And cool."

With two more swallows he drained his glass and set it on the table. Sighing again, he prepared to go. The poacher in the hat stepped down the bar directly alongside him. He turned to face the man.

"Can I help you?"

"Buy you another round, Captain?" The poacher had an American accent.

Stephen took the chance to look the man over more carefully. He was young and now, from up close, it was obvious he was definitely an American. He had that square-shouldered posture and cocksure attitude Stephen knew so well. Stephen didn't like this fellow countryman much, but instinctively he knew he had to respect the power the man's natural arrogance gave him.

"All right," he said, "thanks."

"Set 'em up, Eddie," the American was slightly surprised by Stephen's acceptance. "I'll have what he's having."

Eddie cringed at the unwarranted familiarity, but didn't notice another of the poachers get up from the table and walk over, this time to a position down the bar to the left. Eddie tried to clue him to the other man's presence by pointing an index finger on the bar in the direction of the new arrival.

The second poacher, another white, was huge, scraggle-toothed and dirty mean looking. The last of the group, a wild-eyed African, a tribesman who must've been the poachers' guide and who looked like he would ask few questions of his clientele, stood at the table but didn't move towards the bar.

"So, Captain," the American went on without touching his drink, "you work on the old preserve, eh?" Stephen took a swig of his drink. "Real nice out there, a lot of good animals."

"Yeah," the big poacher to Stephen's left piped up, "good for nothin'." Stephen didn't look at the big one but turned again toward the American.

"Is that thing there with you, buddy?" he said.

The American's eyes flared.

"We're all together, pal."

The big poacher stepped up close to Stephen's left shoulder. Eddie fidgeted behind the bar. Nothing more was said for a few moments and Stephen, downing the rest of his drink, set his glass on the bar, wearily wiped his blazing forehead and again stepped out as if to go. The American blocked his way.

"Move aside," Stephen said quietly.

The American didn't move.

"Have another one, Captain," the poacher said, "be neighborly. We'll only be around on business a couple more days. Show us some Kintara hospitality—and respect."

The big poacher laughed and Stephen felt a strong surge of heat that wasn't fever related.

"No, thanks." Beads of sweat ran down his forehead. "You've had all the hospitality you'll get here, and all the respect you're due. You're not fooling anybody around here with your 'business.' We've seen you out on the plain."

"Free country, ain't it," the big poacher said from behind Stephen.

"That's good that you seen us out there," the American sneered. "We're not hiding."

"Doubt that you would know how."

"So what if you've seen us," the big poacher growled. "You plannin' to do something about it?" Stephen continued to ignore this big one.

"Say, let's knock this off, fellows," Eddie said. He was probably having visions of his bar smashed to pieces. He no doubt much preferred its present configuration. "C'mon, all of you, have another drink. On the house."

No one listened to Eddie. Stephen now stood with his back squarely against the bar, the American and the big poacher in his peripheral vision, the tribesman looking back at him from across the room.

"We came to get that last one," the American said matter-of-factly.

"At least his horn." The big one said thickly.

"Maybe you will and maybe you won't."

"You plan to stop us?" the American challenged. "In your condition? Aren't you just a little on the weak side from all that sweatin' I see you're doin'?" He reached out and gave Stephen a little shove in the chest.

Without thinking, Stephen unleashed a right hand that shocked him with its power. He hit the American squarely in the cheek and dropped him to one knee, stunned. Suddenly, then, as he somehow expected and was surprisingly prepared for, he was besieged. The tribesman raced across the room to join the big poacher and they leaped upon Stephen, pushing him to the floor and hammering his head and upper body with wild, sharp blows.

He struggled to regain his feet and from his knees delivered a left hook that split the tribesman's mouth and broke his nose. The big one grabbed his arms in a full Nelson just as the American recovered enough to reach the fight and slam a hard right into his face, followed by a tremendous kick to the groin.

Stephen bent in pain and the big one brought down both hands in a chop to the back of his neck. The American delivered a hurried, glancing kick to the side of Stephen's face that cut him and numbed the inside of his mouth. The big one pulled his head back, jerked him to his feet and held him upright while the tribesman and the American punched him, bloody and swollen-faced into unconsciousness.

As he went out, Stephen heard Eddie's voice as if from deep inside some distant cave and then the far away sound of a police horn. His last thoughts were futile curses for the bloody fever that had weakened him and for the animal called the last one, the single creature that had brought these violent men to Kintara.

—

Once, in a better time, Stephen read in an old document he found back on the preserve, the rhino herd at Kintara had been the largest in the region. As time passed, however, and more progress and development came into the land, with the subsequent destruction of their living habitat, the herd was thinned to a fraction of its former size.

Presently, it consisted of three females and the remaining male, a gnarled old specimen everyone called "the last one." The last one was just that. He was, as best anyone knew, the last living male rhino in the region. In his youth he had sired dozens of offspring but in later years, when the herd-thinning became critical, he seemed able only to produce female children. There were no males to carry on the strain.

The keepers guarded him as closely as possible. He bore wounds from at least two poaching attempts but there was continued hope he would sire his heir, another male to carry on the line and rebuild the herd.

But the last one didn't seem up to the task. His production, as was natural for advancing age, had slowed down measurably. In fact, there hadn't been a birth in the park in over two and a half years and that baby was nearly immediately shipped off to a waiting animal park in Europe—the extra money being used to help keep Kintara afloat. Yet, despite the efforts of the local keepers, the poachers seemed destined to prevail—the rhino in Kintara, and probably everywhere, would pass forever from the earth.

The presence of this latest group of poachers in the park, the hostile American and his two equally violent companions, only served to heighten the sense of urgency about the safety of the last one and the sense of malevolence that more and more fouled the clean air of the preserve.

With his fever, Stephen seemed especially sensitive to the malignancy of these outlaws in the apparently close-knit, yet isolated and vulnerable community that was Kintara. He knew the coming of the poachers was to be the struggle he had feared for so long. It was a struggle that, even in good health, he feared would be beyond him, be his ultimate defeat. He feared the end.

—

In the early daylight after the fight in the Kudu, Stephen spotted a distant cloud of dust moving towards the preserve's main waterhole and he knew the time had come. Hitting the accelerator and shifting into fourth gear, he pushed his beat up vehicle to its limit—it coughed and rattled down the dried up dirt road like some old man in the last throes of emphysema.

Ahead, the dust cloud had vanished behind a small group of hills but he drove on, battling the bouncing, jerking steering wheel all the time. He knew that the old male rhino, the last one, must be at the waterhole and he was hell-bent to get there before the poachers. Still, every rocky bounce hurt his bruised hands and the hot, dusty air stung his lacerated and swollen face. And the unending fever seemed to be draining what little bit of extra strength and mental alertness he had and would need in the coming crisis with the poachers.

Roaring up over the top of a hill where the road veered sharply to the left, he was suddenly and to his great surprise, right in the middle of an ambush. Several large logs had been stretched across the road ahead of him and as he braked to avoid them he heard the sound of one of his tires blowing, quickly followed by the unmistakable report of a high-powered rifle.

As he fought the skid on the soft dirt, swerving back and forth out of control, he could only feel the ludicrousness of his situation and what a miserable failure he had shown himself in this conflict with the poachers.

"Damn it to hell." The vehicle slid into the logs and rolled over onto the driver's side, useless and lifeless like some great extinct mechanical beast.

Pulling his wounded, feverish body from the wreckage, Stephen found that, luckily, only his left shoulder had been bunged up. He searched for and found his rifle, then used his CB radio to call for help. As he called, he painfully loaded the weapon and honestly hoped he would get a chance to use it.

"They're heading for the waterhole," he told the crackly voice on the other end of the radio, "after the old rhino. They've disabled my vehicle but I'm going after them on foot. I only hope I can get there in time."

Dropping the radio into the front seat, he headed towards the waterhole as fast as he could. He felt hot and tired and he was tremendously thirsty. Now he only wanted to finish this thing that the poachers had begun. Nearing the final rise in the road before it dropped down and ran along within a quarter-mile of the waterhole, he heard the shot. There was just one. It echoed across the plain and up into the small hills.

"Damn you," he cursed and again, "damn you."

He cleared the rise at a ragged jog and spotted the poacher's vehicle near the waterhole. There they were, all three of them by the downed animal. Dropping to one knee, he raised his rifle to fire but his hurt left arm was so weak it afforded little support in aiming.

With sweat pouring off his face, he fired an errant round somewhere in the direction of the men and worked the bolt-action for another shot. More quickly than he could believe, the poachers answered his fire—dust spewing up all around him, followed by the terrifying crack of their game rifles.

Yet he sought no cover. Instead, he stood up and fired off the remaining five shots from his clip, then clumsily pulled another magazine from his pocket and shoved it into the rifle. He fired twice more before his fogged senses told him he was getting no return fire, then he heard the sound of a motor revving up.

"Come back," he yelled into the hot air, "you lousy bastards."

Rushing down the hill and into the scraggly bush towards the waterhole, he wasted two more rounds firing at the sound of the poachers' vehicle as it pulled away. When he reached the clearing where the last one lay, he saw the poachers again. They were sitting in their Land Rover on the opposite side of the bank laughing at him. The big poacher waved something at him, but he couldn't tell what it was through his fever-blurred eyes.

Kneeling beside the last one, he painfully raised his rifle to fire a final shot at the poachers. Anticipating the move, the American steered the Land Rover away from the waterhole and into the burnt-out bush just as the round sailed ineffectually, though closely, over their heads.

Tossing the rifle down in disgust, he knelt beside the huge rhino, the last one. The last male survivor of what was once the pride of the Kintara game preserve. Battered and defeated, Stephen felt a deep sense of shame and humiliation for having allowed the animal to die so at the hands of the poachers. A lonely and undignified death for what was once a magnificent and vital creature, a beautiful, healthy species. Looking up, he could see dust far off in the distance.

"Too late," he thought of the approach of the other wardens, "too late."

But then, to his great surprise, the last one stirred. The animal was not dead. Stephen knelt to him quickly, inspected the thick folds around the animal's shoulders. The poachers had only hit him with a tranquilizer round. The last one stirred again, rolled towards Stephen, who quickly moved out of harm's way. A rhino, even a tranquilized one, could do some serious damage up close.

Walking around the animal, he saw what the poachers had done in the time it had taken him to reach them and then drive them away. The last one's top, shorter horn, had been severed cleanly at the base. Sliced flat against his prehistoric head. The bottom, larger horn was intact.

He started to curse, then leaned back his head and laughed instead. The sound carried on the air of the great preserve, floated across the parched plain. It was a laugh that he knew—as it came fully unbidden—owed at least as much to madness as it did to joy.

—

Stephen came back to consciousness with a start. By the time his head cleared and his blurry vision had sharpened once more, he realized he was still in the bathroom at the Kansas City Zoo. Sighing, he hurriedly finished his business and got out of the stall.

Pausing to wash his hands, he looked into a mirror hanging above the wash basin. The reflection he saw there was a little disappointing. He was not a big strong, muscular game warden. He was just himself. Same old Stephen.

And yet....

Hustling outside, he was surprised to see Tom and Lisa waiting for him. He hoped it hadn't been for long.

"I'm sorry, guys," he said, the strength and firmness in his voice even catching him off guard, "I hope you haven't been waiting for me long."

"Naw." Tom raised an eyebrow. "Only about five minutes or so."

"Are you okay?" Lisa looked into Stephen's eyes. "You didn't have one of those fainting spells in there, did you?"

She was so smart. So observant. He thought the world of her even if she could never, ever feel the same about him.

"No," he lied.

"Another five minutes and we were going to call the trash department to go in there and hose you out, though," Tom joked.

"You sure you're feeling okay?" Lisa repeated.

"I feel really good," Stephen assured her.

"You ready to head out, then?" Tom again glanced at Lisa. "Call it a day?"

"No, I don't think so. I still want to check out the African exhibit."

"Really?" Tom said.

"It's still a bit of a walk," Lisa reminded Stephen.

"I'm up for it. I want to see the rhino...yeah, I especially want to see the rhino. Might be the last one."

"All right," Lisa said. "Let's do it."

"It'll be a lot later when we leave if we do this," Tom reminded Stephen. "I didn't think you were that keen on going through the 'hood on our way back, especially not if it's late."

"Ah." Stephen dismissed the concern. "It's fine around here. The people are fine. No problem."

"Okily dokily then," Tom said.

Stephen marched on ahead of his friends, leading the threesome off towards the African exhibit. Tom and Lisa hung back a few paces watching their buddy striding purposefully before them.

"Amazing," Tom said quietly, "what's gotten into safari boy up there?"

"I don't know, but I like it, whatever it is."

"All of a sudden he's cool, calm, and collected. Mr. Relaxed."

"Sure seems like it."

"Heck." Tom quickly accepted the moment's new, if perhaps ephemeral reality. "Who knows what's up with him or for how long it will last, but I don't see any reason to look this gift horse in the mouth."

"Nope." Lisa picked up the pace to catch up with and walk alongside Stephen. "No reason whatsoever."

DEATH SHIP

Tom Harris decided to take the scenic route to the Maifest celebration clear across the state in the little green hamlet of Hermann, Missouri. Stephen was slumped in the back seat directly behind Lisa Backman, his other best friend from work, and the unobtainable object of many of Stephen's worldly desires, who occupied the rider's seat in Tom's two-year old Toyota 4Runner.

From Nevada, they had driven east to Highway 13, turned north to Warrensburg and from there east again to Sedalia. At the intersection of Highways 50 and 65, near the Missouri State Fair Grounds, they turned left, again north, and drove on to catch East I-70 about fifteen or so miles north of Sedalia. From there it was a straight run to Hermann and the little group settled into relaxed travel mode.

By the time the travelers reached the long, rich bottomlands of the Missouri River, as the road wound by Rocheport—once the temporary headquarters of Civil War guerrilla leader Bloody Bill Anderson—Stephen was getting a little thirsty and hungry.

"I don't know about you guys," he yawned as they zoomed along the interstate towards Columbia, "but I need something to drink and it wouldn't kill me to have a little snack either."

"The water's right there in that little cooler behind me, you big doofus," Tom said. "If you moved your feet, you'd knock it over."

"Ha, ha." Stephen yawned again.

"Are we keeping you up?"

"Five a.m. is early to get on the road."

"You two," Lisa said, "are about as silly as any two guys I know."

"Tom started it," Stephen said.

"Weenie boy." Tom snickered.

"Nerd."

"Dork."

"Stop it," Lisa ordered. "The two of you put together wouldn't make one good half-wit."

"Oh, you got me." Tom dramatically put his right hand over his heart. "Done for."

"That was a good one," Stephen said.

"Puh-lease," Tom groaned.

"Thank you, Stephen." Lisa favored Stephen with a beautiful smile. "There may be hope for you yet."

"You're welcome." Stephen puffed out his chest.

"Glad I'm wearing my hip boots," Tom said. "It's getting so deep in here I won't be able to get out of the car when we get to Hermann."

"Drive." Lisa wagged a finger at Tom. "Just drive."

—

It was mid-morning when the threesome reached the exit for Hermann, home of the annual Maifest, a German-inspired celebration of beer, polka music, and heavy, oily sausages. Taking Exit 175 off the interstate, they drove across an old-fashioned steel bridge and then through the lushly green, tree-filled countryside leading to the tiny burg about a dozen or so miles south of I-70.

Nestled on a forested hillside, Hermann had a story-book, European quality to it. It seemed out of time and place, a mountain village with stereotypical narrow streets, gingerbread houses, and friendly, welcoming people.

"I love it here already," Lisa said, practically before they had found a parking space on a side street and gotten out to soak up the local ambiance.

"Yeah." Stephen looked around at the busy streets and central plaza filled with tourists, locals, and ubiquitous food and drink vendors. "This is great."

"Let's get something to drink," Tom suggested. "I could down a stein or two right about now."

"Where should we go?" Stephen said. "I'm hungry, too."

"Gee," Lisa said, "that's a tough one. Find food and drink at the Maifest. However will we be able to do that?"

"Very funny, smart butt," Tom told her. "Here's a place right here. Krautwurst Sandwiches, Beer. Think that'll do me."

"I'm all over that," Stephen said happily.

"Pigs," Lisa said.

"Let's do it." Tom led the way.

Tom and Stephen went for the krautwurst sandwiches - huge bratwurst sausages laid out on a kind of hoagie roll sliced in half and then buried beneath a mound of sauerkraut topped with vinegar for Tom and a mayonnaise-based salad dressing for Stephen. Lisa settled for a plate of fried potatoes. All three of them got extra-large plastic cups filled with a mellow Pilsner beer.

"Whoa," Tom said, about halfway through his krautwurst. "My eyes were way bigger than my stomach with this thing."

"Told you so, piggies." Lisa had only nibbled around the edges of her potatoes and barely taken a full drink of beer.

"No wonder you're so skinny." Tom set his sandwich down on the picnic table they'd managed to commandeer under the bright, nearly cloudless sky. With the sun nearing its zenith, the day was warming up quickly.

"She's not skinny," Stephen said between big, messy bites of his sandwich. "She's in great shape. I mean …."

"Thank you, Stephen."

"Pathetic," Tom said. "Both of you."

Stephen tried to laugh with a mouthful of sausage and sauerkraut.

"I want to go down to this little winery I saw on our way in," Lisa announced. "Either of you guys want to join me, or are you too busy stuffing your faces?"

"I think I've had about all I can hold," Tom said. "I wouldn't mind going."

"Stephen?"

"Mmph, mmph."

"I'll take that as a no." Lisa said. "Or that you'll catch up to us when you get done stuffing your pie hole?"

Stephen wagged a finger at her to indicate the latter option.

"Come on as soon as you can."

"You can have the rest of my sandwich if you want it," Tom said.

"Othay. Beth air minute."

"God he's articulate," Tom said. Lisa laughed.

As his friends walked away, Stephen continued devouring his sandwich but no sooner than they were out of sight he started feeling funny.

"Ugh." He belched, holding a hand over his mouth. He glanced over at an older man at another table nearby. "Sorry."

"You okay?"

"Uhh," Stephen essayed a reply. "Ate too much."

"There's a lot of that going around."

The man seemed like an amiable sort. He had some remainder of what must've been a German accent, which seemed appropriate for the Maifest.

"You sure you're all right?" the man inquired again.

"Sure." Stephen realized he had lost so much energy that he was in the process of lying down on the seat of his table. "I feel fine."

He closed his eyes and took a deep breath. When he exhaled, everything went completely black.

—

Stephen woke to the metallic pounding of what he surmised to be a nearby engine. It was loud, this engine. It smelled of hot oil and gave off considerable heat. He could feel the grimy, oily heat emanating from this machine, practically searing his skin. The engine's large pistons churned up and down, up and down, their relentless sound hammering against his eardrums.

He kept his eyes closed for several moments more, hoping that if he simply didn't open them and look around that wherever he was would go away, and take that machine with it. It didn't. Finally, he gave in to the heat, the odor, the relentless sound, and slowly opened his eyes.

"Hell." He looked around at his immediate surroundings. "I'm in hell."

"Of course you're in hell," a nearby voice yelled at him above the engine, surprising Stephen so fully that he almost leapt off the small cot that he found he had been lying on.

He screamed involuntarily.

"Knock that off," the owner of the voice said gruffly. Stephen turned to see who the person was. It was a short, filthy, greasy, grimy, rough-looking character who did not seem to be used to polite company or conversation. "Get up off your lazy butt and get busy."

"You can see me?" He held out both hands, palms up.

"Of course I can see you," the man said in a decidedly British accent. "What do you think, you lazy, bone-idle, jackanapes?"

"Hurry up with that coal," another man stood at what looked like a large oven at one end of the large engine that continued to pound away, "and stop jibber jabbin' wit yourself." This man had a distinct German or at least East European accent.

"This cannot be happening." Stephen closed his eyes again, but when he reopened them, the two men and the merciless machine were still there. "Crap."

"Help me with the coal and hurry up before Druck gets back and gives us all a good tannin'."

"Who's Druck?"

"You'll find out soon enough, now get to work."

He followed the man into a large compartment off the engine room filled to the ceiling with chunks of coal. He and the man grabbed shovels and filled a contraption that looked like a wheelbarrow but was larger and squarer.

When they returned to the other room, a third man popped in and immediately began to apply oil from a large can onto the moving parts of the engine. With each application, small amounts of the fluid were flung from the machine out onto the floor making little rivulets and pools around the thumping engine. The new man produced a filthy rag, already mostly wet with oil, and swiped the cloth ineffectually over the spills around the machine.

"Who's that?"

"Seamus," the British man said, "he's the oiler. And the wiper. The boy who was wiper disappeared two days ago."

"Disappeared? Where did he go?"

"More coal," the German called above the din of the engine, cutting off any answer Stephen might have gotten to his questions. "Get me more coal."

"Here it is, damn you," the British man yelled back. "Throw it into your hell hole. And go with it yourself, if you will."

"Shaddup, Howard," the fireman growled. "We're all in hell. In the belly of the profiteer's hell."

"Ha," Howard the Britisher growled back, a hard smile playing on his lips, "your words give you away. I know who you are."

"I'm nobody." The German's aggressiveness seemed to abate slightly. "I'm everybody. This is hell."

Howard and Stephen stood to one side as the German shoveled the new coal into a hot boiler, the steam from which clearly drove the powerful engine. Seamus, the oiler, continued his duties as if no one else was in the engine room at all. Neither the German, nor the Brit, nor Stephen.

"You think I don't know why you are in the guts of this pit of hades," Howard said to the German.

"Stop your bloody pesterin'," the German countered, sweat running down his coal-blackened face. "Who are you? What do you want?"

"Ah, there you are," Howard replied. "I want nothing. It's me that's the nobody. You, however, my fine Bavarian friend, are somebody. It's who you are that matters."

"Not true." the German paused momentarily in his work. "I am only a worker being ground beneath the pounding engine of capitalism."

"Listen to him," Howard said to Stephen, "he's a bloody red. Worse than a Bolshevik."

"How can that be of matter to you?" The German looked all around Howard to see who he was talking to. "It's not for you to know, or any man, who I am."

"Why can't you simply admit who you are? What are you hiding?"

"What?" The German's eyes darted evasively from side to side. "I am not hiding anything."

"Then who are you?"

The German tossed a shovelful of coal into the boiler as Seamus, the oiler/ wiper, flitted by at his repetitive tasks. "If you must know, my name is Torsvan."

"Torsvan." Howard turned to Stephen. "Do you believe this man?"

"Why do you talk to yourself?" the German said. "You act crazy."

"Crazy am I?" Howard said. "I know you're a liar."

"Who's a liar?" A booming, coarse voice exploded from behind the arguing men.

Howard and Stephen practically jumped out of their skins with fright. Seamus the oiler kept working as if nothing had happened at all. Torsvan, the fireman, stoked the oven with coal and didn't turn around.

"I said," the voice growled out the question once more, its ferocious tone echoing throughout the claustrophobic environs of the engine room, "who is a liar?"

This time Stephen turned to see who the speaker was. He wished he hadn't. The voice belonged to a massively thick, foul-looking man whose face was contorted into wrinkles of anger and disgust, a clear statement of personal opinion about his fellow man. This had to be the engine room's first mate. The one Howard had warned him about.

"Druck?" Stephen said to Howard, as quietly as he could.

"Druck."

"What did you say?" Druck snarled.

"N— nothing," Howard eked out.

"Cowards," Torsvan growled under his breath.

"I heard that, Torsvan."

Stephen noticed for the first time that Druck carried a long, round piece of wood in one hand—it resembled nothing if not a policeman's nightstick. The first mate raised it threateningly towards Torsvan but the fireman kept shoveling coal and did not turn to face the harsh first mate. Getting no response, Druck turned on Howard again.

"Get in there and get more coal," he ordered, "or I'll put more bruises on your malingering backside. You've felt it plenty times before. You know I'll do it again. Now move. If this engine loses steam I'll beat the lot of you and cut water and rations. You'll do what you're told or I'll bring you in line or kill you. One or the 'nother, makes no difference to me."

Howard and Stephen scurried to the coal room and began rapidly filling another of the squarish barrows. Druck stayed in the hold for another moment, cursing and threatening the workers. Then, apparently satisfied with his performance, he turned and vanished back into the bowels of the vessel from which he had apparently come.

When he was sure the man was gone, Howard shook his head. "Bastard."

"He's really scary." Stephen said.

"He's a bastard." They wheeled the new barrow up to the fireman.

"And you are a coward, you crazy self-talkin' limey," Torsvan declared.

"You've not felt his club like I have." Howard pulled up his ragged, torn shirt to reveal several bruises and contusions on his upper body.

"My God." Stephen was horrified. "He did that to you?"

"To me, to anyone he thinks challenges his authority. Look at poor Seamus, he never talks. Druck beat him senseless. He's like a machine himself now."

Stephen watched the oiler/wiper go about his silent, near robotic-like tasks. Seeing the poor devil made him shiver with fear again.

"Druck is like a dictator," he told Howard. "A cruel, capricious devil."

"That he is, lad," Howard said, "that he is."

"Must you do this talking to yourself?" Torsvan paused in his work to lean on the coal shovel. "This place is hell enough without your madness."

"I may be mad," Howard responded testily, "but I don't try to hide who I am. I'm not afraid to be myself."

"Go away coward." Torsvan shoveled again. "And take your jibber-jabberin' with you."

"You're just as afraid of Druck as I am."

"The next time he raises his club to me, we'll see." The fireman spat.

"Easy to boast when he's gone."

"Go away." Torsvan shoveled harder. "Get more coal and leave me alone."

"I still know who you are." Howard grabbed the empty barrow they'd first brought to the fireman.

"Go to hell."

"We're already there," Howard said. "We already are."

"Why do you fight with Torsvan so much?" Stephen wheeled the barrow back to the coal room. "Why do you care who he is? I don't understand."

"He thinks he's better than everyone. Has his nose in the air."

"What about?"

"He's a writer, an actor, an artist," Howard explained, making each of the nouns sound like a gangrenous disease. If Stephen had been less unsettled he might have even laughed at the way the coal hauler described Torsvan. It sounded so old-fashioned, so early twentieth-century. Something you would have heard in the 20s or 30s probably. "A radical, an anarchist, a red."

"How do you know that? Did you know him before?"

"Aye, I did." Howard rested from the work. "And he would probably brain me with his shovel if he knew how much I know."

"Would he hit this Druck guy, too?" Stephen pictured the fireman dashing the first mate's—indeed all of their—brains all over the engine floor. That was a scary image.

"Who knows? Torsvan is an excitable man. Perhaps he would."

"All because he's trying to hide who he is? What did he do?"

"Ah." Howard tossed a couple of shovels full of coal onto the barrow. "It's a peculiar story. I learned it from a mate down at the custom house before we crewmates was shanghaied onto this floating hell of a *Totenschiff*."

"*Totenschiff?*"

"That's the name of this steamer from hell. The *Totenschiff*."

"Oh."

"Our name-shy fireman," Howard went on, "has an interesting past. He's a Bavarian, like I said, an actor, a writer. His real name, at least his last name, was Marut. He became mixed up in a communist rebellion about five years ago that failed. Nothing worse than your revolution failing on you. Losers aren't treated well. My friend told me Marut and the other leaders of the rebellion were arrested and brought before the authorities. He was to face a firing squad. They had shot several others but Marut, maybe helped by someone, escaped. Escaped his sentence. Escaped his own death. After that he made his way to England, where he changed his name and now pretends to be someone else."

"What did he do to warrant a death penalty? I mean specifically."

"He published a radical journal. It was revolutionary, calling for the overthrow of the government. Here." He pulled a ratty piece of paper out of his pocket and handed it to Stephen. "This is part of a cover from that journal."

"*Der*—uh, uh—*Ziegelbrenner?*" Stephen pronounced the German title haltingly. "What does that mean?"

"Der Ziegelbrenner—The Brickburner," Howard translated. "See how the brick pattern on the cover was once a bright red. A commie all right."

"What's he doing on this ship? Why would he be working in this hell hole going to who knows where."

"Mexico. It's Mexico we're going to. I believe he's escaping German agents still out to kill him."

"This sounds familiar to me now somehow," Stephen scratched his head. "There's something about all this."

"More coal," Torsvan's voice roared from behind. "Stop talking to yourself and get me coal."

"All right, all right," Howard hurriedly filled up the barrow and ran it out to Torsvan.

The German immediately began shoveling the coal into the boiler. Howard grabbed the other barrow and pulled it away, backing towards the coal room. Stephen followed close behind. Just as they reached the door of the storage compartment, Druck suddenly reappeared. He made a straight line for Howard, club upraised.

"I warned you, you lazy British bastard."

Howard let go of the coal barrow and ducked just as Druck's club slammed down past his head and banged against the barrow. Howard raced out into the engine room and got behind the oiler Seamus, who continued his mechanical, robotic-like work. Stephen hid behind the coal barrow and held his breath.

"Get back, Druck," Howard cried out as the vicious first mate ran towards him, stick held high and threatening.

"I'll teach you, you slug-bum," Druck bawled, "I'll beat the work back into you."

Howard maneuvered Seamus around as protection from Druck. The traumatized oiler seemed void of life, his eyes glazed over as if he were now seeing the black void of a meaningless world—which perhaps he was.

The relentless Druck kept coming, hustling around one side of the engine, arm drawn back to strike. Then, just as Druck brought down his club to render a vicious blow against Howard, there was a rapid movement from behind, followed by a metallic thud loud enough to be heard above the churning engine. Druck spun away and the club fell from his hand. He fell past Seamus head first into the engine, against the pounding, grinding pistons churning up and down, up and down.

In a heartbeat, Druck's mangled body bounced back onto the floor of the engine room—blood draining from front and back head wounds—limp and lifeless. Behind him, shovel still lifted, was Marut, eyes crazy-wild, filled with bloodlust.

"My God," Howard said above the declining sound of the slowing engine, "you killed him. You murdered him."

"Not murder." Seamus the oiler shocked even Marut by speaking. "Self-defense. He would have killed us all. He saved us. Self-defense. Saved us."

"Good lord," Howard exclaimed.

From his hiding place behind the coal barrow, Stephen stood, not thinking of where he was or how he had gotten there. He started walking towards Howard. To his surprise, Marut looked over and apparently caught the movement.

The coaler screamed, rushing around the engine towards Stephen, his bloody-edged shovel pulled back like a war club.

"Howard," Stephen yelped, "stop him. Help."

"Stop, Marut," Howard called to the coaler. "Don't. Don't."

But it was too late, Marut ran at Stephen like a madman, swinging the shovel.

"Help me," Stephen cried, as the shovel came down powerfully, right at his head. "Help me," he repeated, but it was too late—all the light from this hellish world had been extinguished.

—

As Stephen slowly worked his way towards consciousness, he became aware of intense heat, of sweat dripping down his back into the top of his undershorts. He felt like he was being baked in an oven. Coughing and spluttering, he slowly opened his eyes to the glaring light of a painfully bright sun directly above him in the clear, Missouri sky.

"Whoa, baby." He averted his eyes.

"Are you okay, son?" It was the voice of the older man he'd talked to before he'd gone out.

Pulling himself up to a sitting position, with the man's help, Stephen realized a crowd had gathered round. Faces moved in and out of the crowd like small moons, some looking concerned, others smiling, some indifferent.

"Here," the older man said kindly, "let's move you into the shade. You're sweating quite a lot."

"Yes." Stephen allowed himself to be maneuvered on the picnic table seat so that the unblocked sun no longer hit him directly. "Thank you."

When the crowd saw that he was going to be all right, they began to disperse, go back to the pursuit of fun, food, and drink at the Maifest. A couple of small children zoomed by, one of them lightly touching Stephen on the knee as he jogged past. Stephen looked up. The child ran on.

"Will you be okay, now?" the older man said again.

"Yes. I'm fine. Thank you, sir."

"Do you have friends here, somewhere, to help?"

"Yes, they've gone over to one of the wineries. I'd better catch up with them."

"Be sure to take your time. Go easy."

"Yes, sir, I will. And thank you again."

"You're welcome."

"By the way, sir." Stephen stood. "Was I out long?"

"Oh, no, just moments."

"That's good. Thank you."

"Good day, then, young fellow. Have fun, but take it easy."

"Bye, sir. I will."

As the man drifted into the large, milling crowd nearby, Stephen sighed and began to slowly walk in the direction Tom and Lisa had gone. On impulse, he reached down and patted his pants pockets from the outside. Something was in the left one. He reached into the pocket and slowly extracted an old, crumpled up piece of paper. Carefully opening it, he let out an audible breath.

"Holy cow." He stared down at the cover of an aged, faded journal. He read the title softly, but out loud, to himself. *Der Ziegelbrenner.* The Brickburner. That's unbelievable."

He took a quick look around the Maifest grounds, imagining for a moment that he would spot the men of *Das Totenschiff* somehow brought into this time, this place. He was overjoyed to see only the faces of happy festival-goers.

"Phew." He blew out a deep breath. "I'm glad to be out of that hell hole."

Repocketing the partial, tattered cover of *Der Ziegelbrenner*, Stephen began to walk more quickly towards where he assumed Tom and Lisa would be. He looked forward to seeing his friends again, to enjoying the pleasure of their company, to being back in his safe, comfortable world.

Living a quiet, mostly uneventful life wasn't such a bad thing when you thought about it. Compared to other lives and worlds, like the hellish one he had glimpsed on *Das Totenschiff,* it could be downright pleasant. He was sure of that.

KRISTALLNACHT

"Why do you keep obsessing about this?" Tom Harris asked to Stephen White during their usual morning break from their usual graphic design work at Animatec.

"Because I don't understand. I just don't get it."

"Don't get what?" Lisa Backman entered the pungent break room, which mingled the odors of old sandwiches, overripe fruit, and stale coffee into an olfactory pastiche of remarkable staying power.

"Stephen's off on another of his brainiac pursuits," Tom said as Lisa grabbed a soda from a rather noisy refrigerator and joined her friends at the table they had commandeered toward the back of the room.

"I'm not a brainiac," Stephen demurred. "I'm just inquisitive."

"Enquiring minds want to know," Tom teased.

"Want to know what?" Lisa took a drink of coke and set the bottle down on the table. "Come on, guys, fill me in."

"Cain and Abel," Tom said.

"Cain and Abel? What about 'em?"

"Stevie wants to know why the Big Guy was down with Abel's offering but not with Cain's. Like it's suddenly the most important thing in the world."

"It's just a kind of conundrum or something," Stephen said. "It's no big deal."

"Have you thought about asking a clergyman?" Lisa suggested.

"Don't get him going." Tom waved his hand. "You'll just make him worse."

"What's the idea anyway?"

"I just want to know why Cain's offering wasn't up to Abel's, that's all," Stephen answered.

"I don't know the Bible well," Lisa said, "clue me in."

"It's from Genesis," Tom told her. "Cain was a farmer and he brought the Big Guy an offering from his land whereas little bro Abel gave like a fatted calf or whatever. The Big Boy didn't go for Cain's stuff and Cain ends up wasting Abel."

"You asked a local church guy?" Lisa turned to Stephen.

"Yep, but all he wanted to talk about was how Jesus made all the Old Testament stuff irrelevant."

"How about a rabbi?"

"A rabbi?"

"You know a Jewish rabbi."

"There's one here in Nevada?"

"No," Tom said, "we don't have a synagogue."

"Uh-oh," Lisa said, "I feel a road trip coming on."

"Go to KC to see a rabbi?" Stephen questioned.

"No way," Lisa said, "Columbia. I happen to know that there's a synagogue there. And Columbia's a lot more fun than KC."

"A lot further, too," Stephen noted.

"I'll drive," Tom offered.

"Road trip." Lisa cheered. "The big three on the road again. Let's do it."

—

Late on a bright, clear Saturday morning Tom drove his Toyota 4Runner down Broadway in Columbia. Lisa sat beside him in front, Stephen in back— acting mildly sullen and disinterested. Suddenly Lisa cried out.

"There," she pointed across Broadway to a buff-colored building. "There's the Temple Bethel."

"A lot of cars there, maybe we should do this some other time," Stephen suggested. "We're right in the middle of their services. Geez."

"No," Tom said, "I see people coming out. Maybe perfect timing."

"Will the rabbi talk to us on a Saturday?" Lisa wondered.

"Well, answer me this. Does the pope shit in the woods?" Tom joked. "Does a bear wear a funny hat?"

"What?" Lisa wondered. "What was that about? You're mixing your religions there, Mr. Sacrilegious."

"Sorry. Maybe a little inappropriate?"

"Geez, you sound like a hillbilly anti-Semite or something."

"Let's not go," Stephen slid down in the seat as Tom pulled into the synagogue and parked towards the back.

Worshippers filed out of the building, visiting among each other briefly before finding their cars and heading back out into the Columbia traffic.

"See that man by the door?" Lisa pointed. "Gotta be the rabbi."

"You do the talking, then," Tom said. "I'm already disqualified and Stephen is acting like a dork."

"No, I'm not."

"C'mon, dummies. He looks like a nice man. He won't mind some visitors."

"How can I help you young people?" the rabbi greeted the threesome as they approached him at the door of the synagogue.

"Are you the rabbi?" Lisa said.

"I am, young lady."

"This may sound strange to you, sir, but we actually have a biblical question for you."

"Why strange?"

"We're not Jewish."

"But you have a question for a rabbi. How may I help you?"

"It's our friend, there." Lisa indicated Stephen. "He has a question about Cain and Abel and our pastor's answers didn't work for him."

"A biblical scholar?" the rabbi said.

"No, sir," Stephen finally said, "it's just like— uh, a conundrum for me."

"We don't mean to trouble you, sir," Tom added.

"No trouble at all. I'll be happy to help if I can. Come, come into my office. We can visit a spell."

"Thank you," Lisa said.

The rabbi's office was to one side of the worship area, which Stephen thought was quite like any other church except for the difference in symbols used. The rabbi invited the travelers to join him in a small glass of wine. The group pulled up chairs around his desk and sipped on the wine.

Stephen thought his wine had an odd, pungent flavor to it but he went ahead and drank it as he listened to the rabbi explain that the Cain and Abel story was best understood as a metaphor and not a literal story.

"But what are we being told?" Stephen felt a little woozy. "What does the metaphor mean?"

"It operates on several levels, the first having to do with how we serve God, how we may please him. Another level, of course, relates to the idea of us being our brother's …. your friend," the rabbi pointed toward Stephen who had suddenly slumped down behind them.

"Stephen," Lisa and Tom cried simultaneously, rushing to his side.

But Stephen didn't hear his friend's concern or feel them lay him carefully on the floor in front of the rabbi's desk. He was drifting away quickly then. The exterior world grew dimmer and dimmer. Finally, he closed his eyes as the light in the room faded, faded to a tiny point. Then all was total darkness.

—

Stephen found himself moving slowly and carefully down a dusty gray street. He was in a sand-colored camouflage uniform and boots. He carried a rifle at the ready and he understood somehow that less than fifteen minutes before an insurgent IED had been detonated under the lead Humvee in his convoy. His ears still rang from that explosion even though the vehicle in which he had ridden was two back in the formation. Immediately after the bomb went off, the convoy came under intense enemy small arms fire.

Now, as he and the rest of his unit, about a dozen men after the losses, scoured the area looking for the attackers, he was in an ultra-heightened state of awareness. With slow movements of his head, he took in the surrounding area. Run down houses made of crumbling concrete or some stucco-like material that he really couldn't identify, a wall mid-way up one side of the street with several of its concrete blocks broken and others hanging precariously out over the road—no doubt a relic from some previous explosion.

The road itself was buckled in several places, a mixture of asphalt and concrete sticking up jagged above the surface. An arc of bullet holes ran across the front of one ragged home. There were no plants or grass to be seen anywhere. The area gave the overall impression of a battered moonscape on earth. There were no civilians, ostensible non-combatants, to be seen anywhere.

For Stephen, everything had occurred in a kind of slow motion since the IED explosion. He was a little surprised that he felt no fear. As he observed the troops behind him, the empty street ahead, it seemed to him that the world turned like it were an old 78 RPM record, like the kind he'd seen at his great-uncle Joe's when he had been just a boy, played at 33 RPM. It was a result, he knew, of his training and of his extended tour experience in the war zone. He was experiencing, putting into practice, what drill instructors called "relaxed focus."

Relaxed focus—it was what the great athletes strove for and what Sgt. Craft, the platoon sergeant, stressed to the unit. You had to be calm, relaxed, in order to fight efficiently. If you were scared or tense, you were apt to freeze up, endangering yourself and all of your unit. So, you had to not freak out when firing started. At the same time, you had to be completely in the moment, locked in on every task that the situation required. This was the focus. Together it was relaxed focus, the tried and true method for success. The great jocks had it, used it, won with it. So did the army.

Now, in that clear zone, Stephen kept his M-4 Carbine at the ready, listened for any communications that Sgt. Craft might send over the helmet headsets—assuming the headphones worked, assuming they hadn't been plugged up as usual by the fine, local sand that played havoc with all equipment—vehicles, rifles, everything.

Across the way, he watched his fellow soldier, Corporal Brown, super jumpy since the IED attack, jerk his head in every direction as he searched for the elusive attackers on the other side of the road. He could see Brown had an itchy trigger finger and that he was close to letting loose with the .12 gauge he loved so much because of the way it fired so fast and the pattern it produced in a 30-40 foot range of absolute destruction.

Brown was as brave as they came, but he tended to be a little high-strung and a little too fast to act. He was not only good with the shotgun and courageous but he had a way of sniffing out trouble. Stephen kept him in sight and stayed alert.

As the two GIs neared the end of a street, where it made a ninety degree left turn into another unseen but no doubt similar road, Brown gave a short wave with his right index finger, signaling to join him on his side of the street. With a look back at the rest of the platoon, now some distance behind them in the street, Stephen slowly, cautiously crossed over.

When he was just a few feet away, Brown waved his finger again, hooking it to indicate they should round the corner into the next street. Stephen held up his left hand, palm out, to indicate a halt.

"What's up?" He sidled up close to his friend.

Brown bobbed his head to the left twice.

"You see somethin'?" Stephen held his hand up, palm out again.

"Cover me." Brown pointed ahead with his finger.

They stepped into the middle of the road and walked slowly towards the corner. Because the road made a ninety degree turn to the left at the corner, neither could see anything beyond the intersection. Stephen moved a few feet further to the right, away from Brown, and brought his weapon up ready to fire just in case they encountered a surprise.

When they reached the corner, he moved a few feet ahead so that they would make the turn together. Brown gave him a thumbs up sign and he returned the gesture. They had each other's backs, he felt, no matter what.

But then, at the moment, the very second they crossed into the next street everything suddenly, with no warning, changed. He felt a strange tingling all over his body accompanied by a shift of ambient air temperature. It got a lot cooler, really fast.

And it was much darker, almost impossible to see after having left the light of the semi-arid Middle East. It was cooler, darker, louder, and filled with people running in every direction. He stumbled slightly, realizing that somehow he no longer carried his heavy army pack on his shoulders.

The people around him were shouting back and forth and at first he couldn't understand what they were saying but he was surprised how quickly their strange speech became clearer until he could completely understand them. It was all odd, yet somehow familiar.

Stepping beneath a streetlight, he could see in the weak illumination of the watery, yellow globe, both himself and Brown. The sight was unnerving. Brown still carried a pump shotgun, but it was of an unrecognizable manufacturing brand and style. As for his own weapon, it too was different. Gone was the M-4, replaced by a thick, heavy rifle, a Mauser according to precise etchings on the barrel.

He also saw that they were dressed in all-black uniforms, a style both foreign and old-fashioned. They wore high, heavy boots that thumped and thudded as they walked. On their heads they wore V-shaped, cloth hats, also black with white stripes along the top creases. On their left shoulders were insignias.

Insignias of the Third Reich.

"My God," he said amid the din of shouting people, all young men, who were racing up and down the street, Todstrasse, a sign on the side of a wall read, "Nazi Germany."

The young men tearing up and down the street also dressed in black, but not in uniforms like they wore. These men appeared to be gangs of civilians, intent on destroying the doors and windows of every shop and residence they could find on the street. He wasn't sure what to do about the general chaos but he instinctively refrained from trying to control the mob.

"Brown," he heard himself call out, "what's happening?"

"Come ahead." Brown raised his shotgun into the air. "Let's find out what these people have done."

"People, what people?"

"C'mon, up here."

Stephen looked across the road where Brown now pointed his shotgun. Next to several buildings whose every window and door had been broken, with glass and wood debris strewn across the sidewalk and into the street in all directions, stood a small shop, a little grocery store with its front door and display windows untouched by the anarchic violence. Fires burned in several buildings nearby and berserkers seemed to be running everywhere. Yet nothing had, to this point, befallen the small grocery.

"Wait," Stephen said, "we don't have to go in. That's not our mission."

"What about the window? What about that?"

"What about it?"

"Star of David."

"So?"

"Look at the wall. Look on the bricks."

Stephen let his gaze drift from the obviously hastily drawn Star of David on the shop's front window to the dirty, once red brick wall of the building itself.

"Juden." He couldn't believe the word even as it left his mouth.

"Juden," Brown echoed. "Now, come on. Inside."

"Take it easy. These are civilians. Not fighters. We aren't here to harm…."

His last words were lost as Brown, shotgun at the ready, opened the shop door and entered the little grocery. He hurried after.

A little bell attached to the top of the door tinkled gently as the two soldiers made their way inside. When Stephen closed the door behind himself he was amazed at how muffled the sound of the rioting outside became. It was as if the interior of the grocery existed on yet another plane removed from the already surreal one outside.

"Everybody out here," Brown, apparently little affected by this strange new world, barked at the people inside the store. He seemed intent on rousting out whoever was in the building. "Out here where we can see you."

Stephen started to say something to calm his friend down, but he thought better of it and just kept a wary eye on the situation. In a moment, there were three terrified people standing before the two soldiers.

The shopkeeper, a short, thin man in a dark suit made shiny by much wear and little cleaning, was bareheaded and his dark eyes, set deep in his hollowed-out face, flitted back and forth nervously between Brown and Stephen. A woman near the shopkeeper's age, maybe mid-thirties, stood to one side with her arms around a girl of about ten. A husband, wife, and daughter—a small, hard-working family; what could they possibly have done? There was no reason to roust them out.

"I don't think there's any reason—" he started to say, but Brown cut him off.

"What is your crime?" Brown held a hand up to silence Stephen's objection.

"Crime?" the man said. "I am only a small grocer, I—"

"Do you know why the people are outside?"

"No. I do not understand it."

"Do you know why we are here?"

"No, sir." The man dared a glance at the woman and girl. Fear was palpable in their eyes.

"Brown." Stephen edged forward with a brief smile for the woman and child, which they seemed too afraid to reciprocate. "This is just a little grocery. Let's go. There's nothing here for us to do."

"Maybe, maybe not. Anywhere can be used as a hiding place."

"A hiding place? For what, who?"

"For contraband, weapons, the enemy."

"But we are not the enemy," the grocer dared interject.

"We'll decide that," Brown told him.

"I'm sure they're law abiding citizens," Stephen attempted another smile for the benefit of the family. The family tried to return the smile. It wasn't working for any of them.

"What's behind that curtain there?" Brown demanded, causing the grocer to flinch. "Is there somebody back there?" He raised his shotgun towards the curtain. "Does that go into another room?"

"N— no, sir," the grocer stuttered.

"You're hiding somebody."

"No. No one is there. No one."

"Really? Then you won't care if I shoot into the room then."

"Brown," Stephen intervened again, "don't do that. There's no reason to do that."

"Please, sir," the grocer begged, "don't shoot. We have nothing. We're hiding nothing. It's only...."

The shopkeeper's words trailed off with the onset of a low rattling sound from the back of the room. The curtains, hanging motionless before, began to move. Brown thrust his shotgun forward, aimed it directly at the curtains.

"No, no," the grocer cried. "Don't."

"Please," the grocer's wife wailed, breaking her long silence. "No."

Brown clicked off the safety on his shotgun. Sweat beads formed on his forehead and his hands shook ever so slightly from the tension.

Without hesitation, Stephen stepped between Brown and the curtain.

"Don't shoot. Wait."

"What?"

"Just wait. Take it easy."

For another few seconds the soldiers remained still, at a high state of alert. Ready for anything. Then the curtain was pushed aside. Stephen let out his breath loudly.

"I told you they were hiding somebody." Brown brandished the shotgun.

"Not hiding," the grocer said. "She's my wife's mother. She was working in back."

"Grandmama," the little girl cried out, holding her arms out for the old lady who stepped from behind the curtain. The old woman looked at the soldiers, couldn't seem to understand their presence in the store.

"Who are these young boys?"

"We were just leaving, ma'am," Stephen told the woman, then turned to the grocer, his wife and child. "We're going now. We're sorry to bother you."

"What are you doing?" Brown demanded.

"Getting us out of here. Come on. These are just shopkeepers."

"We don't know that."

"Outside." Stephen motioned towards the door. The grocer and his family watched the soldiers' every move.

"What if they have somebody or something else back there?" Brown pointed his shotgun back at the curtained off area. The old grandmother instinctively ducked.

"There's nothing back there," Stephen put a hand on Brown's shoulder and turned him around. "Let's get out of here."

While the little grocer's family stood wide-eyed, watching, he hustled Brown to the front door and then outside. On the street again, people still ran in every direction and the noise was a shock after the unexpected quiet of the grocery.

"They could've been hiding someone," Brown said petulantly, as they stood side by side on the sidewalk. "We could get in real trouble if they were. We have a mission here."

"You're right," Stephen agreed. "I'll go back in. I'll take care of it."

"I'm going with you."

"No, I'll do it. Stay here and keep an eye on this crowd."

"You better do it."

Stephen went back into the store. The little family had gathered in the middle of the grocery and looked up in terror when he reentered.

"Not to worry. I'm not going to hurt you."

"What do you want?"

"Get behind the counter and stay down."

As soon as the family complied, Stephen gave the store a fast once over. Stepping up to one wall, he swiped his free arm through a row of canned goods and knocked them to the floor. He repeated the swiping on another row and then knocked a few things off the main counter. He saw the family hovering behind the counter in fear.

Then, to make it good with Brown outside, he stepped back and fired a round from his rifle into the ceiling. Dust and small pieces of wood and plaster dropped down onto the floor. Someone let out a brief cry, the old grandmother perhaps, but then was silent.

"Let that be a lesson to you." He backed out of the store, nodding politely at the grocer who stared back in utter amazement. "Never forget it."

Outside, he closed the door behind him, blocking Brown's attempt to peer into the store.

"Well? You really gave it to them?"

"I gave it to them."

"Yeah." Brown impulsively slammed the butt of his shotgun through the grocery front window. The glass made a tinkling sound as it fell onto the narrow sidewalk.

Moments later, they heard another noise, one more grating to the ear than the softly falling glass. It was a loudspeaker. The voice on it sounded authoritarian, crisp, disciplined. The voice called to the rioting berserkers, exhorted them to further action, to more destruction.

"Let's go." Brown bolted in the direction of the loudspeaker.

"Damn it," Stephen said. "Wait up."

But before he could reach the next street corner, Brown made a sharp right turn and disappeared.

Stephen chased after him as fast he could run. Without looking, he reached the corner and made that same sharp right turn.

There was a sudden increase in light, almost a flash it became bright so rapidly, and he found himself back on the hot, dusty street where he and Brown had been only moments, or was it years, before. Stumbling off a curb and letting out a little cry, he caught himself before falling under the weight of his heavy pack.

"What the hell?" he said. "What was that?"

"What was what?" Brown called from a few feet up ahead on the street.

"Brown?"

"Who the heck else?"

"I thought— ah, just forget it."

"You goin' weird on me or something?"

"Just walk on."

"I don't know about you." Brown turned around and resumed his slow, cautious walk up the dusty street. "Hey," he almost immediately yelled.

"What? What?"

"I just saw a civilian run into that house up there." He pointed up the street.

"Where? Which one?"

"On the right. Second house. With the funny writing on the side."

"Was he armed?"

"Couldn't tell, he was moving too fast. We better check on it."

"All right," Stephen agreed, "but take it easy. Follow procedure."

"Relaxed focus."

"That's exactly right."

As Brown made his way towards the house, they heard a helicopter somewhere nearby. Probably a medevac chopper—and beneath that was another, sharper, sporadic, cracking. There was a firefight going on no more than a block or two away.

"Hurry up, Brown."

"I'm goin' into this place," he called back just as Stephen picked up a squawky voice on his headsets.

It was Staff Sergeant Craft.

"Repeat," Stephen said into his helmet mike.

The response was lost in static. The sound of gunfire outside the muffled world of the helmet increased in intensity and rapidity.

"Brown," Stephen yelled, "let this one be. Forget this house."

"What? Why?"

"We've got to get back to the unit. They're under fire."

"But we can't forget this civilian. He could come back and kill us."

"We can't do both. We've got to help the platoon. This place ain't right."

"You got a feeling or somethin'?"

"Come on. Enough of this house. Stay on mission. Hurry."

"Okay," Brown acquiesced. "If you feel it, I'm with you."

Hustling down the road, they had gone less than thirty yards when the house they had been standing in front of blew. The explosion knocked the door off its hinges and flung it out into the street. Seconds later, a cloud of dust and smoke roiled out of the opening left by the bomb. They stopped to look back.

"Jesus Christ," Brown exclaimed, "we'd a been blown to hell back there."

"Didn't happen," Stephen said, emotionless. "Never mind that. Hustle up. They're still firing over here."

"How did you know, man? How did you know not to go after that civilian?"

"I don't know." Stephen puffed from their double-time pace. "I had this sense we'd done something like that before, you know. Didn't you feel it?"

"I didn't feel anything. You must've had some kind of weird deal happen to you or something."

Stephen began to form an answer but a sudden fatigue came over him. He staggered, dropped to his knees in the street, slowly slumped over on his side. The last thing he saw was Brown looking down at him. He wanted to tell his friend that it would be okay but just as he began to speak, everything went dark around him.

He completely lost consciousness.

—

"Some kind of weird deal or something happens to him every now and then," Tom said as Stephen slowly came awake.

"Don't move," Stephen heard Lisa say, then the face of the nice rabbi appeared above, moon-like and benevolent. Stephen tried to smile.

"Take it easy, there, young man," the rabbi cautioned. "We thought we lost you for a minute."

"He scares us half to death with these … episodes." Lisa held Stephen's right hand and softly patted it. "We have to watch him like a hawk when we go on excursions."

"Well, he's lucky to have such good friends. Lucky indeed."

"Don't try to sit up," Lisa told Stephen, who made a feeble attempt to rise.

"How long have I been out?"

"Just a moment or two," Tom said.

"I think I want to go home now." Stephen let Lisa help him to a sitting position.

"Sure, pal," Tom said. "We'll go back."

"Take a moment," the rabbi advised, "let your head clear, get your strength back, then you go home. Don't rush."

"Thank you, sir," Lisa told him. "You've been quite kind to us."

"I'm not sure I helped with your biblical conundrum, but it's been a pleasure meeting you young people."

"It's a metaphor," Stephen said, "not literal. It tells us how God wants us to worship and love him. I got hung up in the literal."

"Well, it looks like someone is back in the land of the living." The rabbi smiled broadly. "Well said, young man, well said."

"Thank you, sir." Stephen stood with Lisa's help and shook the rabbi's hand. "Sorry for my little moment there."

"Think nothing of it."

"We'd better get him back home, sir," Lisa said.

"Of course. You young people have a safe trip home."

The rabbi walked the three friends to the door and ushered them back out into the bright light of the mid-day.

"Come visit us any time. You're always welcome, here."

"Thank you," Lisa said.

"Goodbye, sir," Tom added.

He and Lisa guided Stephen to the car and got him situated comfortably in the back seat.

"Ready, Freddy?" Lisa asked.

"Ready." Stephen sighed.

Lisa and Tom exchanged worried looks again.

"Just sit back and relax," Tom said. "You rest. I'll drive."

"Maybe you need to see a doctor about these spells when we get back home," Lisa suggested.

"Yeah, maybe you should," Tom agreed.

"Thanks guys," Stephen said, "but I'll be okay."

"We worry about you, you know," Lisa said.

"I appreciate it. You guys are great friends."

"Well, just rest now," Lisa added.

"You bet."

Stephen turned to look out the window and sighed again. Lisa glanced at Tom. He shrugged.

Within a few minutes, they had maneuvered through the streets of Columbia and were back out on Stadium Boulevard nearing the I-70 exits. While Tom and Lisa concentrated on acting like they weren't concerned about Stephen, he was discovering something odd in his shirt pocket.

Digging down, he felt a squarish piece of what felt like glass. Slowly extracting the object from his pocket, he checked it out, turning slightly toward the door and keeping the object out of Lisa's sight. Tom was too busy driving to notice his behavior.

Turning the object in his hand, which in fact was a piece of glass, he saw lettering on it. He angled the glass so that only he could see what was written upon it.

"J... U... D," he read silently, resisting an urge to whisper what he saw on the glass. Below the letters was part of a white triangular shape, perhaps a star.

Juden, he thought, the Star of David, just like on the window of the little store he had seen when he had gone away. Gone where? The piece of glass and its partial symbol and lettering caused him to feel a chill run up his spine. He shivered involuntarily and looking up, saw Lisa leaning back from the front seat intently watching him.

"What you got there, tiger?"

"Oh, nothing," Stephen looked away, pocketing the piece of glass.

He leaned to one side and snuggled against the soft cloth of the back seat. Tom and Lisa briefly looked at one another again but said nothing. Stephen released a long tired breath. The car sped along the interstate, the Missouri countryside passing by in a rich, verdant blur.

CANOE TRIP

The Elk River at the extreme southwest edge of Missouri ran quick and full. Late spring rains filled it nearly to the banks, covering low-water sand bars and submerging jagged tree-limbs that could potentially destroy an unsuspecting tourist's canoe.

Stephen White, who had reluctantly agreed to go canoeing with best friends Tom Harris and Lisa Backman, rowed from the back of one canoe. Tom was alone in a second canoe while Lisa, the unrequited object of Stephen's helpless desire, sat in the front of their canoe.

"Keep us in the middle of the current," she called back for what must've been the twentieth time. "Stay away from the snags and those eddy's by the shore."

"I'm trying." Stephen huffed and puffed and slapped the oar into the water as if trying to flatten some poor fish that might have strayed to the surface.

"And row smoothly. Out, down, pull, up. Repeat. You're fighting the water too hard. You're just going to wear yourself out."

I already wore myself out, Stephen thought, not daring to admit to Lisa that he had no idea how to row a canoe and was in fact totally useless at basically all physical skills. A guy just couldn't admit something like that to a girl like Lisa Backman.

Not only was she pretty and smart, she was in top notch physical shape and kept herself that way by exercising and doing things like rock climbing, running, bicycling. All the activities that Stephen didn't know how to do and couldn't if he had. He could never hope to have a girl like Lisa, but, oh, what a wonderful thought.

"Stephen!" Her sharp cry brought the mostly sedentary software engineer out of his reverie. "Look out for that limb over there to your right. We're going to hit it."

"Yikes," Stephen squealed, almost dropping the oar in a wild, uncoordinated effort to propel the canoe out of harm's way.

The canoe, drifting in the current despite his best efforts, lightly scraped the offending tree branch. The sound was akin to someone dragging their fingernails down a chalk board.

Lisa turned toward him when they finally cleared the tree limb. "Stephen, you've got to give me that oar or we're going to get in trouble here soon."

"I'm sorry. Here. I'm just no good at this canoeing business."

"It's all right. I'll take it for a while. You worked hard there."

"Thanks."

As usual, Lisa had found a way, with a simple smile and change of tone, to extricate Stephen from an unpleasant situation. She always seemed to do that for him. It was another of the reasons why he couldn't help but care for her. She was a genuinely nice person. He often thought, in fantasy-like visions, that he would do anything—even something heroic—to defend and protect her.

—

"Hey, guys," Tom called as the sun began to drop well behind the trees along the banks of the Elk River. "Look up ahead there. That big sand bar would be a great place to camp for the night."

"I see it," Lisa called back. "Looks good. Let's put in over there."

Tom expertly rowed his canoe onto the pebbly shore of the sand bar, climbed out and drug it from the water. Lisa steered herself and Stephen close to Tom's canoe. With Stephen's extra weight, however, their canoe did not so easily reach the shore. She jumped out of the boat and with Tom's help tried to drag Stephen and the canoe onto land.

"Wait, guys, let me hop out."

"Go for it." Tom had never seen Stephen hop out of anything before, much less a canoe. He wanted to see this.

With a rolling, tumbling motion, Stephen tried to exit the canoe but caught one of his boots on the outer edge and fell on his back with a painful-sounding thud. Luckily, he landed mostly on sand, and the impact only temporarily knocked the wind out of him.

"Are you okay?" Lisa bent over him where he lay red-faced between the two canoes.

"I'm...fine...," he wheezed, "just dandy."

After setting up camp, the friends made a small fire, warmed up some quick-fix camping food and after filling themselves sat around the fire drinking from a bottle of red wine Lisa had brought along.

"Mighty tasty, vino." Tom held up his small plastic drinking cup.

"Thank you." Lisa raised hers in return.

"Oh, yeah," Stephen chimed in, even though he hadn't touched a drop yet, "real good choice."

"Here's to us." Lisa again raised her cup. Tom and Stephen followed suit.

"This is what I call really roughing it," Stephen said a few minutes later.

"Oh, yeah." Tom said. "Just like the Osage of old, huh?"

"Right." Lisa chuckled.

"Well, sort of." Stephen backtracked, digging for an old energy bar he found in one dirty corner of his backpack. He brushed off a couple of gritty places on the bar and despite its less than savory appearance began munching away.

"I read that the country around here was Osage hunting grounds and on down into Northwest Arkansas," Tom added.

"Yes," Lisa said, "and the Shawnee, Delaware, and western Cherokee."

"Cool."

"Why do you suppose the Delaware would be way out here?" Stephen finished the dirty power bar. "This is a long way from the east coast."

In his mind, he imagined a band of ferocious-looking warriors, faces painted, wearing feather bonnets and headdresses, carrying spears and bows and arrows. It was an awe-inspiring vision.

"Same reason as always." Lisa said, "encroachment by white settlers."

"Tha's turrible," Stephen slurred. His mouth and tongue seemed to be going numb and he was suddenly sleepy.

"Turrible," Tom imitated him with a laugh. "Are you drunk just looking at the wine?"

Stephen tried to wave Tom off but he could barely lift his arm. Lisa leaned forward to look into his eyes.

"Not again. Stephen are you okay? Is something wrong?"

"Buddy, what's up?" Tom reached over to steady Stephen.

"Sleepy," he said slowly, his big body drifting backwards as if unable to withstand the force of natural gravity. "I— feel— vur— sloppy."

Tom and Lisa made sure he didn't fall and hurt himself. But he was a goner. In the next moment, he was on his back, eyes closed and completely out of it, lost to the world.

—

When Stephen opened his eyes, the camp and river beyond were covered in a low-lying, thick gray-white fog. Even as he struggled awake, he was aware something was wrong.

"What is it?" His blurry vision made out Tom's form coming toward him.

"I can't find her."

"What?"

"Lisa's not in camp. I called for her but there was nothing."

Stephen stumbled to his feet. Tom helped steady him.

"What do you mean? Where did she go?"

"I can't tell... wait, hear that?"

Stephen listened intently. He thought he did hear something.

"That's her voice," Tom said, "she's out there in the woods somewhere. Come on."

Just beyond camp, the fog-filled forest was thick with trees and underbrush. They stopped every fifty feet or so to listen. Once or twice they thought they heard her call again. Going on, they finally came out into an elevated clearing. In the thinning but oddly sparkly and mildly electrified fog, what they saw stopped them in their tracks. Down below in the gray mist was an Indian village.

"What is that?" Stephen was dumbfounded, but Tom acted as if it were as normal as everyday life.

"Listen." He held up a hand to his ear. "She's down there."

Stephen was about to ask where "there" was, when suddenly Lisa appeared in the middle of the village with a crowd of native people surrounding her, chanting and crying out.

"This can't be happening." Stephen took in the collection of animal-skin covered teepees below that constituted the encampment. The men, women and children who surrounded Lisa in the center of the village were partially clad in cloth blankets and fur. The predominant color seemed to be red.

"Shh. We've got to get her out of there. There's no telling what these savages have planned."

"Savages?" He'd never heard Tom say anything like that in his life. Not in their world anyway. "What are you talking about?"

"Our only chance is to surprise them," Tom suddenly produced a large hunting knife.

"Wh—where did you get that?"

"They took her into that small teepee. You create a diversion and I'll sneak down, cut the teepee open and bring her out."

"What planet did you just come from? Cut open a teepee? Make a diversion?"

"Hurry." Tom hustled off to the right into a thicket.

Stephen was trying to figure out what kind of diversion to create when one of the Indians in the camp below spotted him. The man pointed a short spear in Stephen's direction. The other braves looked up the hill.

"Uh-oh," Stephen groaned.

Several of the Indians broke from camp and charged up the hill towards him. He turned and made as fast a retreat from his position as his lumbering body would allow.

"Help!" He flailed his arms in the air as he ran clumsily back into the woods.

It took the Indians all of twenty seconds to catch Stephen and they roughly knocked him to the ground, several of them hitting him with sticks and clubs to count coup.

"Ow." He put up his arms to protect himself.

Several of the warriors drug him to his feet. They pushed him, heavy as he was, toward a close-by tree and were about to tie him to it when new shouts were heard from the direction of the camp. He looked over his shoulder and saw Tom and Lisa running helter-skelter right toward him and the braves.

There must be something he could do, he thought, racking his stressed out mind. A plan, rudimentary though it was, popped into his head—all the more remarkable for its simplicity.

"Ha," he yelled at the Indians.

The ones closest to him jumped back. Maybe the large white thing was more dangerous than it looked.

Lowering himself into what he thought was a Brian Urlacher-like middle linebacker football stance, he raised his arms—fists clenched—to his sides and let loose a blood-curdling yell. The warriors threw up their hands in surprise. A couple of them backed up.

With another screeching cry, he lowered his shoulders and slammed his big body right into the braves. They were caught completely off guard. Like a human bowling ball or a runaway panel truck with four flat tires, Stephen crashed through the Indian men, knocking most of them flat on their backs. The ones not knocked down hid behind a nearby tree. The white thing was clearly insane.

Stephen stumbled on then, into the undergrowth with Indian spears, arrows, bone necklaces, and bows flying in every direction from his crazed assault. Off to his left, Tom and Lisa went rushing by heading for the canoes and the presumed safety of the river.

While the native warriors labored to gather themselves and their weaponry and regain some sense of dignity, Stephen continued his pall mall, headlong bull rush towards the river. Several yards from the water's edge, he began losing his balance and with the still slightly confused Indians as his witnesses he tumbled forward and fell.

Rolling down the embankment like an asymmetrical rock or lumpy cardboard box, he banged and crashed all the way down to the shore. When the fall stopped, he was looking directly at the end of one of the canoes. Tiny waves of water lapped against his nose.

"Ooph," he grunted.

Before he was barely able to right himself, Tom and Lisa grabbed him and tossed his lumpy body into the front of one of the canoes. Lisa hopped in after him and with Tom in the other canoe they rowed furiously out into the river and towards the heavy fog. As they went, flailing their oars, an occasional arrow whistled by, landing harmlessly in the water beside them.

—

While Tom and Lisa kept up their prodigious rowing, Stephen hunkered down and did the only thing he could think of to make the threatening scene around him go away: he closed his eyes.

In what seemed like mere seconds, he heard Lisa call his name. Oddly, she didn't sound scared or breathless from rowing, not even the least bit stressed.

"Stephen," she repeated, "wake up. Time to get going."

"What?" Stephen spluttered, waving his arms about.

"What are you doing?" she said.

"I'm… uh, not in the canoe?"

"Uh, no, we're in camp. We need to load up and row on to the pickup point."

"Oh." He slowly rose, noticing there was a heavy morning fog hanging from about the middle of the river over to the far shore. "We should stay out of that fog over there."

"Stay out of what?" Tom walked over from his canoe.

"Stephen thinks we should avoid that fog bank," Lisa said, with a knowing nod to Tom.

"Why? It's just a low-lying cloud. That's all fog is."

"Trust me on this one. Just this one time, all right?"

"Sure, buddy," Tom winked at Lisa.

"I'm serious."

"Okay." Lisa said. "We'll stay out of the fog. Happy?"

After a quick, light breakfast, they loaded up the canoes and pushed back out into the Elk River. Tom took the lead and stayed just at the edge of the fog. Lisa, rowing her and Stephen's canoe, followed suit. Stephen rested in the back of the canoe, keeping a close eye on the fog.

Several minutes down river, he impulsively reached into his pocket and pulled out part of a broken bone necklace, just like the kind Native Americans often wore. He looked over the fragment of necklace and considered showing it to Lisa. Something told him to keep this find to himself. He re-pocketed the necklace just as she turned around to look at him

"What you got there, river boy?" She gave him one of her 14-carat smiles.

"Nothin'." Stephen let the bone necklace slide back down into his shirt pocket. "Nothin' at all." Lisa turned back to the rowing.

Leaning back again, Stephen watched the fog drift by as Lisa expertly kept the canoe beside the low-lying river clouds but not in them. Occasionally, he would give the bone necklace a furtive rubbing between his fingers.

By mid-morning they were off the river, loaded back up in Tom's car and heading home to Nevada. Stephen figured he would show Tom and Lisa the bone necklace he found at a later date—just not right away, not today. He would save that for another time.

HOSTAGE

On a quiet Sunday morning, under a clear blue sky and a bright, warm sun, Stephen White huffed and puffed his way up a steep bank above the Marais des Cygnes River. He was in a forested region not far from the Missouri-Kansas border and headed toward a cave he had explored the previous fall.

It was in this cave that his "spells," as he liked to call them and only then to himself, had begun. He had first experienced what he believed were hallucinations in the cave. Initially, he had seen Images and visions of a distant pre-human and human past, but then, and far more terrifyingly, he had what seemed to be an actual encounter with outlaws of the Civil War era.

Associating the scary episode with a mushroom sandwich he had eaten that day—he assumed they had been inedible toadstools rather than good mushrooms—this time he decided not to take any chances and had eaten a bland breakfast of eggs, toast and milk. He waited a good half hour to make sure he was having no reaction to his meal before he loaded up a backpack and took off for the Marais des Cygnes, which meandered west to east several miles north of his hometown of Nevada, Missouri.

Stopping to get gasoline at a convenience store on the edge of town, he decided to play everything safe. He bought a large bottle of water—ensuring that the cap had not been broken—and then a Snickers bar and a health food power bar, again checking that their wrappings were factory-sealed. Satisfied that all was well, he drove on to the Marais des Cygnes. He easily found the crossroad off Highway 71 that led to several dirt roads which he followed out to a dry, flat area behind a cornfield where he left his 1987 white Ford Bronco not far from the river.

Now, as he neared a cave he had only partially explored, he was feeling good. He'd brought some knee pads for crawling around inside, worn one of his older long-sleeved flannel shirts—they were always his favorites—to protect his elbows and remembered to bring a small miner's light attached to an elastic band that fit comfortably around his head. He was ready not only to go back into the cave today, but was ready to explore its inner-most regions, even if that meant getting himself dirty and pushing his mild case of claustrophobia a bit.

"All right," he said out loud when the cave entrance became visible several yards ahead of where he struggled out through a thicket of green brush. "Found it again."

The cave, its entryway dark against the greens and browns of the terrain surrounding it, looked for all the world to him like a large mouth gaping out of the countryside. It seemed to smile, perhaps beckoning him, beckoning him to enter into its dark, dank recesses behind the welcoming facade.

"It looks like a big mouth," he said, "calling to me to enter it." A light shiver passed through his body but quickly faded. "I'm not afraid of you," he told the cave, "I'm coming in and I'm going to explore every bit of you today. No fear. Yeah, that's it, no fear."

Just as he remembered, the cave entrance was about twenty-five feet across and over six feet high at its tallest vertical point just off center of the opening. The ground immediately inside was dry and bright brown in color. It looked just as soft as it had when he had easily dug in it before.

Also as he recalled, he could see back into the cave at least forty or fifty feet before it faded into darkness. Approaching the back of the primary room in the cave, he could see, as he had on the other visit, what might be small openings leading to more rooms beyond this front section.

"I'm gonna see it all this time," he said, the sound lightly echoing off the interior walls of the cave. "Every last bit."

Pausing for a moment, he allowed bits and pieces of his first exploration of the cave to play in his mind.

He remembered that when the images began that fateful day last fall, he first thought he had just gotten some dust in his eyes; but it was more than that. He had seen flashes at first, then shadows, causing the hair on the back of his neck to stand up. He recalled suddenly feeling hot and sweaty. His legs wobbled and he felt nauseous, disoriented. The shadows flitted, raced by, seemingly in all directions. He had slumped down, sick and scared to death.

He had tried to make the images go away by closing his eyes but when he looked again the shadows had become recognizable forms. He saw pigs running along the walls of the caves, ethereal-like, something akin to holograms. They ran on either side of him, rushing silently along.

Then more images came rumbling through the cave, out of the cave, into it. There were other animals, deer, bear, small creatures, too, followed by upright images—men. Short men who moved in the cave, hologram-like still, going about the business of their lives. Then they were gone, replaced again by animal images.

After some time, the animals left and a different group of men appeared in the cave. Men with long hair, wearing animal claw and tooth necklaces—and women, too. He saw them chanting without sound, dancing without song, living without solid form. Then they too were gone.

Slowly, then, a new sensation had begun. He heard sounds coming from the back of the cave. Familiar sounds, and smells—of coffee and bacon cooking on an open fire. And suddenly they had been all around him. Talking, laughing, arguing.

There were maybe a dozen of them, dirty, poorly dressed, ragged, so thin their coats hung on them outsized, ill-fitted. They carried pistols stuffed in holsters on their hips, tucked under leather belts that held up their worn pants, stuck down inside their cheap, leather boots.

These men were outlaws, bent on crime and vengeance. And he was right in the middle of them. Propelled then, by curiosity, by strange fate, to experience a terrifying raid with these hard and bitter men, he saw killing and brutality he had never imagined before. In the end, mercifully, he had awoken—alone, safe, back in his own world.

He had not forgotten the things he saw that day, however, not the animals, not the cavemen, not the native peoples, and certainly not the adventure itself, nor the rusted, Civil War-era pistol he had found but never told anyone about. Not even Tom Harris or Lisa Backman, his best friends. He shared most of his life with Tom and Lisa, who worked for the same computer graphics company, Animatec, back in Nevada.

The three companions did many things together, talking about their lives, their dreams, their hopes, but he had never told either of them about his first experience in the cave. And he had been circumspect about the other "incidents" that had occurred to him, even when he had had one of these "experiences" in the presence of his friends.

Now, undaunted by the past he shared with this old cave, Stephen made his way into its dark inner recesses, towards what appeared to be, as it had seemed last fall, small openings perhaps leading to other parts of the cave. It was altogether possible that there were other rooms beyond this main one, rooms that might be hiding a treasure trove of artifacts, manmade and otherwise. At the least, he imagined, there could be incredible crystal or other rock formations in such a place as this.

"Aha." His voice again echoed lightly in the cave. "Found you."

Ahead and slightly to the right of his position was a hole at the back base of the cave. In the poor light he couldn't tell if it was going to be a big enough entrance for him to squeeze through but he was hopeful. Slipping on his caving headband light, Stephen knelt and aimed the beam at the hole. It looked like a tight squeeze but he might be able to make it.

Taking a deep breath and crossing himself for good luck, he wiggled through the hole. It went fine at first. He was moving along well and feeling confident. But then the passage began a short curve and his big body began to scrape against the walls of the little entryway. Then, just as he was about to panic, he suddenly spilled out, a drop of maybe only a foot or two, into an open space. Rolling into a sitting position, he directed his light around his new surroundings.

"Yes." He was now in another large cave room, one that was perhaps half as big as the large outer cave. "Yes."

In this inner room, he quickly discovered the air was unexpectedly hot and stuffy. Sweat formed on his face and trickled down slowly, like a grainy oil instead of natural perspiration. After a moment or two of adapting to the new ambiance, he had thought it would be cool and wet further inside the cave rather than the opposite, he began a tentative exploration.

For some reason his caver light didn't seem to be particularly strong inside this room but he was still able to discern occasional rock formations hanging down above his head. Despite the weaker illumination, he took a small rock pick out of his backpack and after digging along the side of one wall was able to discover a small finger of quartz, which thrilled him. He picked up the glassy quartz and cleaned it with his fingers.

"Most excellent," he proclaimed. "Really most excellent."

After another fifteen minutes or so of unproductive digging, he was thirsty, needed a drink.

"I'm getting thirsty," he declared to the empty cave, "I need a drink."

He reached into the backpack, pulled out the bottle of water he'd purchased at the convenience store, felt the cool beads that had formed on its plastic exterior. Unscrewing the cap, he took a big swig.

"Ugh." He tasted the dirt of the cave floor that had attached itself to his hands and then been mixed with the water when he drank. He wiped his mouth only to taste more of the dust. "Darn it. That don't taste good." Still, it was surprisingly hot inside the cave so he forced down another couple of drinks, spitting grains of muddy cave soil out as he did.

After taking a couple of bites of his Snickers bar and resting several minutes more, he decided to crawl on. He leaned forward to get on his knees but immediately realized something was wrong. He couldn't seem to lift his body from the sitting position.

"Not good," he mumbled. "Not good at all."

He tried to kneel again. He failed again. He simply didn't have the energy for it. He was getting more tired by the minute, even sleepy now. And even though he still had his spelunking light on, the cave seemed to be getting slowly darker and darker.

"Not again," he slurred. "Why does this keep happening? Oh, damn."

With one last effort, he tried to stay awake, to get to his knees, but it was no use. He was unable to move his body. Tiring of the effort, he simply slumped back. His eyes closed against his will. The room seemed to be totally void of light. In a matter of a few seconds more, he was completely out.

—

After what seemed no longer than it takes for the eye to blink, Stephen returned to consciousness, but there was something wrong. Really wrong. He could see absolutely nothing. No light reached his eyes. It was blacker than pitch, blacker than the deep heart of a night before light had been invented. Terrifyingly black.

"Yaiaee, help. I'm blind."

But out of that blackness came no help, rather the opposite as he was knocked hard against his left shoulder by some solid object.

"Ow." He tried to reach for his offended arm. But he couldn't, his arms were tied behind his back.

As his eyes adjusted somewhat to the dark, he realized that his face was encased in some heavy, densely opaque cloth. That was why it was so black, there was a hood over his head, and he was in a sitting position in some kind of rough, uncomfortable chair.

"Oh, my God," he exclaimed into the cloth, "what's happening? Why is this thing on my face."

"Shut up," someone in the darkness yelled at him, just before he received another blow from the unseen solid object—a rifle butt? The voice had a decidedly foreign accent to it.

"Is this a hood on my head?" He meekly tried to move his bound hands.

"Be quiet," the same unseen voice said, "or you will go to your last reward."

"I … I can't breathe," he gasped, beginning to hyperventilate.

"Shut up, calm down. You're not blind and you can breathe. Calm yourself."

Stephen tried to do as he was told, but it was difficult. He had never had a hood over his head before, much less one that was so thick and dark as this one, and he'd never had his hands tied behind his back before either. What was going on? Who were these people—for despite his inability to see, he was sure there were others around him besides the man who had spoken to him.

When he was able to bring his emotions under some control, he began to breathe less rapidly, more easily, much quieter. He listened carefully, heard several voices speaking not far from where he was—across a room perhaps.

The voices all sounded male and they were speaking what he guessed was a middle-eastern language. The man who had spoken to him, though, at least knew some English. Stephen dared to speak again.

"Where am I?" His voice, from under the hood, sounded muffled even to him.

There was shuffling nearby where the voices were and then he knew for certain he was surrounded by these as yet unseen men.

"I have warned you," the same man as before said. "Keep quiet. You are in real danger. The others want to kill you now. It is possible I cannot stop them."

"Who— who are you?" he stammered, against the man's instructions. "Where am I?"

"Infidel," another voice suddenly yelled next to his head. The epithet, delivered with an extremely heavy accent, was almost immediately followed by a hard hand punch to his stomach.

"Oh." He doubled up involuntarily. Strong hands grabbed him and forced him back into an upright position. "I'm sorry."

There was a flurry of loud talking in the language he could not understand. He felt something push against the side of his head. It was hard and metallic. They're going to kill me, he thought, wanting desperately to see his captors, to speak to them, to find out what was going on. But he knew better now, had learned a quick lesson. He held his tongue, said nothing.

While he listened to the men talking, moving about outside his black world, he tried to gather himself. He focused on the here and now. He had controlled his breathing and was beginning to deal with the darkness of the hood, although occasionally it seemed there was some vague light finding its way through the heavy material that covered his face. He tried to tell how many men were in the room with him, but there was so much movement he couldn't be sure whether there were three or four, possibly more. Perhaps they were moving in and out of the room.

And where was this room? Apparently in some sort of house—that would be a safe assumption. At least two of his captors, he wasn't sure what to call them, knew some English, the one man quite a bit. Possibly he would be able to talk to them at some stage.

Whatever had happened, whoever they thought he was, it was surely just a mistake and as soon as he could explain himself they would let him go. Sure, that was it, they would see that he wasn't whoever they thought he was and just let him go. They were bound to listen to reason. They wouldn't just be cold-blooded killers—would they?

"We are not," the voice of the better English-speaker suddenly sounded next to Stephen's left ear, causing him to practically jump out of the uncomfortable chair in which he sat uncomfortably, "cold-blooded killers. If that's what you think. We are soldiers, fighting for our freedom, our faith, our country. If you do what we tell you, you may perhaps live."

"Who are you?" He attempted to quietly aim his voice only at the man who spoke. "I mean no disrespect."

"It does not matter, but if you must, call me Nazr, that's as good a name as any other."

"Thank you, Nazr. Thank you."

"Be quiet, the others are coming back."

Moments later, he heard the movements of several people as they came in and out the room. He wished they would go away so that he could speak to Nazr alone, explain to him that this was all some kind of terrible mistake, that he wasn't a threat to these men nor was he their enemy or whatever it was they thought about him. In a short while, things quieted down again.

"Nazr," he dared to say softly, "Nazr, are you there?" He prayed for luck, that the ones who had hit him were not there.

"Yes."

"Where am I? Where is this place?"

"You know."

"No, I don't."

"You're in a safe house, not a mile from your cursed Safe Zone."

"My Safe Zone?"

"Yes."

"I don't understand. Where is this place, this house?"

"I've told you enough. Be quiet. The others will be back soon enough and they do not believe in talking with an infidel. They may kill you."

"Why? What have I done?"

"You are here, that is enough."

"Will you please take this hood off, it's so hard to breathe and so dark?"

"Not yet, not until later, when the others say."

"Why do you speak English so well?" Stephen tried another tack. "The others don't."

"I studied in the—" Nazr began but quickly stopped.

Of a sudden, there was the rushing sound of men coming into the room again. Stephen tensed and shut up. He could sense that Nazr had moved away from him. It was time to lay low.

—

After what seemed like interminable minutes, hours perhaps, he gleaned from bits and pieces of conversation—how he understood he did not bother to ask—that he was a prisoner of Sunni insurgents somewhere in Baghdad. This made no sense, but it had become all too clear what his captors had in mind for him—death. Then, while he was considering his likely fate, and to his utter surprise, the hood was quickly removed from his head.

"Can you breathe better now?" Nazr, from somewhere behind Stephen, spoke in a surprisingly gentle tone.

"Yes." He checked out what he could see of his surroundings before him. "Thank you."

It was a sparsely furnished room. Besides his chair, only two straight-backed wooden chairs and a small, worn couch could be seen. The house seemed to be built of something like stucco and he made out a long crack along one wall and smaller cracks in the two corners of that wall.

It was night outside, although the dark drapes over the only window in the room would have let precious little light in had they been open anyway. It was a classic "safe" house, he imagined. Exactly the place where a captive could be held without anyone bothering to look for him.

"Nazr," he said to his guard, "I am not your enemy. I have done nothing to you or to your people."

"The presence of the infidel army in our holy lands makes you our enemy."

"But I'm not the army. I don't want to be in your holy land."

"Nevertheless you are."

"It's a mistake. Please let me go."

"I cannot do that."

"But this isn't right. I can tell by your accent that you must've spent time in the U.S. You can't really hate us, the people."

"I had American friends, this is true," Nazr admitted, "but that was before, before you invaded and destroyed my country. Now you are my enemy."

"But...."

"Hush, the others return."

Seconds later, the room again filled with insurgents. This time Stephen could see them all. There were four of them. All appeared to be young, although their faces were hidden behind dark scarves that were wound around from the neck to just below the eyes.

They were all thin, nervous, armed to the teeth. One man carried what must've been a hand grenade launcher, another a small hand-held rocket. The tallest of the group, who carried the grenade launcher, saw Stephen looking at them and detached himself from the others to come stand directly in front of Stephen.

"What are you looking at?"

Stephen recognized the man's voice as being the one who had first called him an infidel and who had apparently punched him hard in the stomach. He tensed up, unconsciously hunching his shoulders forward in preparation of receiving a blow. At least for the moment, the expected blow was not forthcoming.

"I said, what are you looking at?" the tall man repeated.

"N...nothing," Stephen stammered.

"You are lucky that we do not kill you now."

"But I've done nothing to you. I don't have anything against Islam. Or Arabs. How can you hate me so?"

"Don't patronize us. For a thousand years you infidels have exploited our land, our people. Desecrated our holy places, defiled our God."

"I haven't. I haven't done anything."

"Liar." The tall man signaled to the others. "Put the hood back on him. Perhaps he will shut up his lies and see his sin."

"No." Stephen tried to resist, but before he could do anything the hood was back over his head.

Moments later, again in the blackness of his sightless world, he heard the men hustle out of the room and, presumably, from the house itself. He waited several minutes more before daring to call out to Nazr, who he assumed the other men had assigned to be his personal guard.

"Nazr," he whispered, "Nazr."

"I am here," the familiar voice spoke, after a long delay.

"Nazr. Thank God you're there."

"What is it?"

"They mean to kill me, don't they?"

"All men must die."

"But I haven't done anything. Whatever they think, I'm not guilty."

"We are all guilty. You. And I."

"But you can save me."

"Only the will of Allah can save you now."

"It's not right. It's not fair."

"You should have thought of that before you came here.

"But I didn't come here, you brought me here," he reminded his captor.

"Your country came. You came."

"Isn't there a way to co-exist? A way to compromise?"

"We did co-exist. Before your western greed and corruption found its way here to our world, to corrupt and exploit it, us. We can co-exist if our sovereignty is respected and you go back to your own land."

"It's too late for that. That's the old way. It's all about globalization now and world markets. The old ideas no longer hold."

"Then we will wage the holy jihad until all infidels have been killed or defeated and driven from our world."

"That's a medieval idea," Stephen said boldly, "from a thousand years ago."

"Hush," Nazr's voice faded, "the others return."

"Wait, Nazr, wait."

But Nazr was gone, or at least out of earshot and speaking range. Stephen heard the other men rustling around nearby. He tensed again. Assumed he was in imminent danger, that death awaited him, could come at any second.

"It is time," he heard the tall man say from somewhere nearby, somewhere in the darkness beyond the captive's hood.

The man's tone of voice sent chills through Stephen's quivering body, but before he could cry out his objection, someone pulled the hood roughly off his head. The tall man stood before him, his face an impassive mask. Stephen could feel, not see, someone standing directly behind him.

"Please," he pleaded with the tall man, "I've done nothing."

"It's too late, no one can save you now."

"Why me? I'm innocent."

"No one is innocent, especially not you."

"What is my crime?"

"You are guilty." The tall man raised his eyes, looked beyond Stephen.

"Who's back there?" Stephen said. "Nazr? Who is it? What are they doing?"

"Nazr?" the tall man cocked his head to one side. "Nazr?"

"He wouldn't do this to me," Stephen asserted. "He knows I didn't do anything. Ask him. Ask Nazr."

"You are mad." The tall man again looked behind Stephen.

"Who is it?" Stephen cried out, "who's behind me?"

Then, in a terrifying flash of heightened awareness and a distorted, surreal slowing of time, Stephen saw the tall man nod his head at the unseen person or persons behind the chair. To his utter amazement, he could hear a swishing sound as an object, without doubt a large knife or sword, was swung down at the back of his neck from behind. He heard the sound of the instrument as it sliced the air behind him, came down with great speed and force, its metallic edges just touching the hair and skin at the back of his exposed neck—then all was blackness again.

—

Stephen woke again to complete darkness, certain he had been beheaded. But he quickly realized he was shaking and cold, not usual symptoms of the Great Beyond.

In a moment, the smell of old soil and musty air penetrated his olfactory system and he determined he had not been killed or sent off to some black afterlife. He was back in the cave where he had been exploring before his recent misadventure or nightmare or whatever it was had happened.

He tried to move and found that his hands were free. He reached up to his head and was overjoyed to find it intact and that no offending hood had been slipped back over it. He let out a deep sigh and stood up quickly.

"Ow, damn," he wailed, falling back into a sitting position and grabbing the throbbing side of his head. "Damn rocks. Jeez."

He carefully lifted his right hand above his head in the dark, extended his arm until he felt the low cave roof directly above him.

"Man, that hurt, son of a gun."

He held his right hand gingerly against the side of his head until the pain began to subside. Slowly he realized there was some light entering the cave room. It was coming from the narrow opening through which he had entered the interior space. At the same time, he remembered the spelunking light he wore. He thought its battery must have run down, but when he tapped the light with his left hand, a shaft of light—albeit a weak one—shone out into the room.

"All right." He gave the sore side of his head a final rub.

On hands and knees, he made a beeline for the passage leading back to the main room of the outer cave. Just as he had when entering the small tunnel before, he took a deep breath of cave air and crossed himself for good luck. Then he rolled his body up onto the foot or so high ledge at the end of the passage and began wiggling through the hole.

This time he maneuvered through the tight curve in the little entryway with hardly a scrape against the cave walls. He was sure of himself now and scrambled through the narrow tunnel, in no time spilling out of the entryway and onto the floor of the main cave.

"Yes." His voice echoed softly against the cave wall. "Yes."

Hurrying towards the cave entrance, he half-walked, half-crawled through the big, dusty room. In a matter of moments, he reached the front and with a grunt stumbled through the natural doorway into the external world.

Outside it was sunny and bright. He squinted at the sky, so blue and beautiful. His head hurt a little yet from the bump he had given himself but he would be okay. He patted himself down for other injuries but only found, in a pocket, the finger of quartz he'd taken from the interior of the cave. During the check he noticed his wrists were sore and when he examined them more closely, saw thin red lines running all the way around both.

He shuddered to think how close that other reality seemed to have been, if it had truly been another reality. All he knew was that he was glad to be gone from there, to have escaped alive. There might not be a logical explanation for the red marks on his skin but he didn't care—the lines seemed to be fading with every passing second anyway. All evidence of whatever happened would soon be gone for good, all that would remain was the fine piece of quartz from the inside room.

Then, in a moment's time, the brief flare-up of fear and residual apprehension from his "experience" was gone. Holding his arms above his head, the finger of quartz in his right hand, he felt a wave of relief mingled with an equal sense happiness flood through, around, and over him.

He was back in his own world, on the steep bank above the Marais des Cygnes River, still alive. Yes, he, Stephen White, was alive. He had not died a captive in some terrible, dark foreign place. He was still flesh and blood—alive.

Overwhelmed by a sense of well-being and the great pleasure of simply living, he cried out to the world around him—a cry celebrating freedom, life, existence itself. He spread his arms wide as if to encompass all that was.

Then he began to laugh, a happy laugh, the elated laugh of those given a second chance in life, of those newly reborn to the world, of those still with time and opportunity to live their lives to the fullest—from that moment on until the last of their days.

On his drive back to Nevada, Stephen considered the "episodes" he had experienced over the past months. They had been mostly frightening and confusing but perhaps something more. Maybe they had taught him something about himself, too, and about the way he conducted his life.

With a rush of positive feeling, he vowed to reconnect with his parents, to make sure they knew he appreciated and loved them. He would try to be a better son and man. He would take Uncle Carl to lunch soon and really listen to his war stories and maybe learn something about life and how to live it.

He would be a better friend to Tom and Lisa and listen to their advice about seeing a doctor concerning his "spells." He needed to find out what was causing them and what he could do to stop them from recurring. And he would dig down inside and find the courage to actually ask Lisa out—on a date. What was the worst that could happen—she would tell him no?

For reasons he did not fully understand, the odd experiences he'd gone through of late had changed him, even if only a little, from the Stephen he had been before. He was stronger now and able to handle things better. So if Lisa turned him down, he could live with that. He might not like it but he could take it now. It wouldn't destroy him like it would have before.

No, he was definitely different. He'd seen things. Learned things. He was ready for whatever might come his way. He was ready to live life as fully as he could—he was ready for tomorrow.

J.B. Hogan is a prolific and award-winning author. He grew up in Fayetteville, Arkansas, but moved to Southern California in 1961 before entering the U. S. Air Force in 1964. After the military, he went back to college, receiving a Ph.D. in English from Arizona State University in 1979.

J.B. has published over 250 stories and poems. His novels, *The Apostate, Living Behind Time, Losing Cotton, Tin Hollow,* and *Mexican Skies*—as well as his local baseball history book, *Angels in the Ozarks,* a short story collection entitled *Fallen,* and his book of poetry, *The Rubicon*—are available at Amazon, iBooks, Barnes & Noble, Books-A-Million, and Walmart.

When he's not writing or teaching, J.B. plays upright bass in East of Zion, a family band specializing in bluegrass-flavored Americana music, and is active in the Washington County (AR) Historical Society, where he's recently served as President.

www.thejbhogan.com

www.ingramcontent.com/pod-product-compliance
Lightning Source LLC
Chambersburg PA
CBHW020911180626
46816CB00007BA/2342